ROSE
RAVENTHORPE
INVESTIGATES

Rubies and Runaways

Janine Beacham

A former journalist, Janine Beacham has written all her life. She has always loved fairy tales and fantasy, and as a child would make up games for her friends to play at school. Janine once entered a competition where the prize was a real-life butler – which partly inspired the secret society of butlers in the *Rose Raventhorpe Investigates* series. Janine lives in Western Australia with her family.

ALSO BY JANINE BEACHAM

Rose Raventhorpe Investigates
Black Cats and Butlers

ROSE RAVENTHORPE INVESTIGATES

RUBIES AND RUNAWAYS

JANINE BEACHAM

LITTLE, BROWN BOOKS FOR YOUNG READERS
www.lbkids.co.uk

LITTLE, BROWN BOOKS FOR YOUNG READERS

First published in Great Britain in 2017 by Hodder and Stoughton

1 3 5 7 9 10 8 6 4 2

Text copyright © Janine Beacham, 2017

The moral right of the author has been asserted.

A CIP catalogue record for this book
is available from the British Library.

ISBN 978 1 5102 0131 6

Typeset in Bembo by M Rules
Printed and bound by CPI Group (UK) Ltd, Croydon, CR0 4YY

The paper and board used in this book are made
from wood from responsible sources.

Little, Brown Books for Young Readers
An imprint of Hachette Children's Group
Part of Hodder and Stoughton
Carmelite House
50 Victoria Embankment
London EC4Y 0DZ

An Hachette UK Company
www.hachette.co.uk

www.hachettechildrens.co.uk

For Rory, with love

PROLOGUE

It was Yorke's coldest winter in living memory. The cathedral roof almost cracked under its weight of snow. Icy winds tore through the skitterways. The cat statues of Yorke, the guardians of the city, were hidden in drifts. Only the black cat on Ravensgate was free of snow. It looked uncannily lifelike, as if it had just shaken off its frosty coat.

A boy bolted down the street. Ragged and wide eyed, gasping for breath, he stopped in a skitterway – an alleyway of Yorke. His heartbeat throbbed in his eardrums. He wiped his nose with his hand.

A black cat leaped down from a windowsill, and

gazed at him with golden eyes. The boy stared back. He was dizzy from tiredness and hunger. That must be why he was seeing things. He thought that cat had been a statue just a moment ago.

He heard footsteps, and glanced wildly about for somewhere to hide. He had to keep running. He had to find help, somewhere.

As he took to his heels, he heard children singing in the distance.

> *If you want to save your skin*
> *Don't let strangers take you in!*
> *You'll go to the undertakers*
> *once you meet the Angelmakers.*

Chapter 1

THE ORPHAN'S WARNING

Rose Raventhorpe felt like throttling her cousin Herbert. Or as she called him, Ghastly Herbert.

She usually adored Christmas. Carols floated through the cathedral, and shop doors wore plump green wreaths. Mrs Standish, the Raventhorpes' cook, made an iced fruitcake that needed two people to carry it to the table. But this Christmas her cousin Herbert had come to visit.

Tall, pale and languid, Herbert was thirteen years old and maddeningly superior. He boasted of his father evicting a whole village to make room for a new mansion. He told Rose to 'stop gabbling foreign languages and speak proper English'. He scoffed at Lord Frederick Raventhorpe's work as an ambassador: 'Your father should go fox hunting, or gamble, like a proper lord.' He even called Mrs Standish's glorious Yorkesborough puddings 'tasteless'. Back in the kitchen, the cook had taken to pounding herbs with unnecessary force. Rose played loud piano pieces to drown out the sound of Herbert's voice.

Heddsworth the butler found Herbert in the pantry tasting from six jars of jam with the same spoon, and smashing the ones he didn't like. 'A London ditch-digger could run a household better than this one,' he sneered. Heddsworth confessed to Rose that he was sorely tempted to put laxatives in Herbert's dinner.

But that was not the worst of it. Herbert had brought his own butler to Lambsgate. Bixby was a sniffy man with heavy-lidded eyes and a tiny moustache. He criticised Heddsworth's napkin-folding, housekeeping records, choice of wines and brand of silver polish. He even refused to let Heddsworth unpack Herbert's suitcase, saying it must be done *his* way.

Rose's black cat, Watchful, hated the visitors. Watchful was an uncanny creature, with the ability to turn into ... well, *something*. Rose still wasn't sure about what she had seen, months ago, in the cathedral. She only knew that some nights Watchful did not sleep on her bed, but went out prowling. Presumably consorting with the other uncanny cats of the city – the statues which kept watch over Yorke.

Now, Rose sat with her family at dinner while the two butlers glowered at each other. Heddsworth had laid the table, but Bixby had tried to change the settings.

'No other butler, no other person, should ever change a table setting, Miss Raventhorpe,' Heddsworth had told Rose, pale with indignation. 'It is an insult.'

As Heddsworth, like many of the city's butlers, was a secret Guardian of Yorke and highly skilled at swordsmanship, insulting him was dangerous. The air crackled with tension.

'Honestly, your butler is a joke,' said Herbert loudly. 'Pay attention, Heddsworth! I wanted cream sauce on my potatoes, not this buttery slop.'

'Shall I take over serving?' suggested Bixby.

'No,' said Heddsworth, glaring at him.

'How are your fencing lessons coming along, pet?' Lord Frederick asked Rose.

'Very well, Father,' she replied.

'I don't approve of it,' said Herbert. 'It's unladylike! You might as well take up boxing.'

Heat crept up under Rose's collar.

'Fencing is a perfectly acceptable sport for ladies,' she retorted.

'Hear, hear,' boomed Rose's father. 'Exercise gives a girl her bloom. She'll be posing for portraits soon, like her mother. What was the last one called, Constance darling?'

'*The Black Swan in the Heather,*' answered Lady Constance Raventhorpe with a proud smile. She touched her perfect coiffure. 'I wore a plaid, a Scottish tartan.'

'Enchanting!' said Lord Frederick. 'Ought to be painted in that dress you're wearing now, my dear. Dashed pretty thing.'

'Oh, I couldn't, Frederick,' cooed his wife. She smoothed her trailing green silk gown; it had a silver lace train. 'I bought it a month ago in Paris. Quite out of fashion now. It's hardly fit for wearing out of the house.'

'I wouldn't want you out in this weather anyway, dear,' said Lord Frederick. 'Jolly bracing, isn't it? Still, a Raventhorpe is never cowed by the elements. I know! You two cousins could have an outing – go to the Mistletoe Service at the cathedral.'

'The cathedral?' groaned Herbert. 'What a bore!'

'Hmph,' said Lord Frederick, put out. 'Yorke Minster's a sight better than anything in London. Heddsworth can go with you.'

7

'I really can't be bothered,' drawled Herbert. 'Pass the gravy, Rose.'

Rose stared at him stonily. 'Pass the gravy, *please*.'

'You heard me, Miss Rose. Or are you going deaf from all your terrible piano practice?'

'Excuse me,' said Rose. 'You didn't say please.'

'Don't be stupid, Rose.'

There was a long pause. 'Please,' said Herbert sulkily.

Rose passed the gravy.

'Don't think you can act like that forever,' sniffed Herbert, pouring gravy over his meal. 'You will have to get used to doing what I say. After all, you're going to marry me one day.'

There was utter silence at the table. Heddsworth froze in the act of spooning mustard on to Herbert's plate. Behind him, Bixby smirked.

'*What* did you say?' gasped Rose.

'You have to marry me,' said Herbert, with his mouth full. 'When we're of age. You're the

Raventhorpe heir, and I'm my parents' only son. You will be the Countess of Dundragan.'

Just at this moment Bixby took the opportunity to joggle Heddsworth's elbow. Mayonnaise splashed on Herbert's front. Herbert yelped.

'Really,' sighed Herbert. 'I do think you should sack Heddsworth. Bixby would be far better. Don't you agree, Rose?'

After dinner, Rose rushed to her father's study.

'Father, you can't expect me to marry Herbert!'

Lord Frederick looked uncomfortable.

'He's my cousin,' Rose cried. 'And he's horrible!'

'Well, yes,' said Lord Frederick. 'But your uncle has always been adamant that the boy marry into the family. And it would give you an excellent position in society.'

'I am *not* marrying Ghastly Herbert!'

'He might improve,' said Lord Frederick doubtfully.

'He won't. Not ever.'

'Well, perhaps we needn't say anything at this point? You're not old enough for marriage yet. And Ghastly – I mean *Herbert*, might find a more suitable bride.'

Rose muttered something unladylike in Arabic.

'Now, now,' chided her father. 'That was poor pronunciation.'

'You didn't promise me away, did you?'

'No, no. But your uncle is very prominent in the House of Lords, and he is a perfect nuisance when I try to change outdated laws. I wouldn't ever push you into an unhappy marriage, my dear,' he added quickly. 'In the meantime, just try to get along with him.'

Easier said than done, Rose thought bitterly.

'And you wouldn't ever sack Heddsworth, would you?'

'Of course not!' said her father. 'Though your mother is rather fond of Bixby, I'm afraid.'

Feeling sick, Rose went to Heddsworth in the kitchen.

'Could you duel him?' she begged. 'You could still teach him a lesson!'

'Tempting as that sounds, Miss Raventhorpe, it would be wrong.' Heddsworth was polishing silver. 'Bixby is not trained in battle as we Yorke butlers are. Nor does he know about our being Guardians of Yorke, or follow the Silvercrest code of honour. No, he would try to provoke me into some outburst, then run off to Her Ladyship and complain about my behaviour, and get me fired.'

'I won't let it happen!' said Rose.

'He'll do his best,' muttered Heddsworth.

'Beastly Bixby,' growled Rose. The kitchen smelled of cinnamon and nutmeg-sprinkled eggnog, but she had never felt so lacking in the Christmas spirit.

'I'm not going to a freezing cold cathedral!' moaned Herbert, the next morning. 'I'll die of pneumonia.'

Rose gritted her teeth. 'You don't have to come

if you don't want to. Heddsworth and I can go by ourselves.'

'Oh no you won't,' said Herbert. 'My future bride can't go about Yorke with only a butler for company!'

'Stop all that nonsense about marriage. I don't have to do anything you say,' snapped Rose.

Heddsworth tactfully intervened. 'I am sure we can wrap you up well, Master Herbert. The service should not take long.'

'Fine,' Herbert huffed.

They climbed into the carriage, and set off through muddy, slushy streets. Local urchins threw snowballs at the carriage. Rose longed to hurl snowballs back, but Heddsworth wouldn't let her. ('Though it would be rather fun, Miss Raventhorpe.')

The cathedral was lit by hundreds of candles and decorated with holly, ivy and mistletoe. Red and white berries shone by candlelight on the altar.

'Beautiful,' breathed Rose.

'I hope there's hassocks,' said Herbert. 'I'm not sitting on a cold pew for an hour.'

Rose heard someone call her name and turned to see her friend Emily Proops – now Mrs Dodge – who rushed up to her, beaming. Formerly fond of mourning clothes, Emily now wore a striped black and green dress.

'How is newly married life?' Rose wanted to know.

'Magical!' said Emily. 'We read Gothic poetry to each other every night. And darling Harry is managing the Clarion Theatre now.'

'Marvellous!' said Rose.

'We'd better find our seats,' said Emily. 'I do wish it was warmer in here. Winter is wonderfully atmospheric, but a cold in the head isn't very dramatic.'

Rose entered the Raventhorpe pew. Herbert pulled his cloak tightly around him, and snapped at Heddsworth for not bringing a hot water bottle.

Rose gazed around the packed cathedral, and spotted her friends from Silvercrest Hall, Bronson and Charlie Malone. Bronson, the only female butler of the Hall, looked as demure as a Sunday school teacher. However, Rose knew the long pocket in her dress concealed a rapier. Charlie, handsome and golden-haired, had a permanent limp from a fencing injury. He winked at Rose, who smiled back.

The service began. The Archbishop welcomed the congregation.

'Today we honour the Mistletoe Service,' he intoned. 'Since medieval times, the people of Yorke have offered forgiveness and peace to the wrongdoers who come here on Christmas Eve. This is a time of goodwill, of gratitude, and of kindness towards one's fellow man. Those who come in a spirit of penitence are asked to approach the altar.'

The congregation waited patiently. Nobody was actually expected to speak. Rose wiggled her toes in her boots, and thought of Mrs Standish's apricot scones with cinnamon cream. There was nothing like hot scones and tea after an out—

Footsteps echoed down the aisle. A wild-eyed boy sprinted towards the altar.

The congregation stirred uneasily.

The boy was ragged and spider-limbed. One eye had been blackened by a punch, and there were other bruises on his chestnut skin.

'My sister's disappeared!' he gasped out. 'From the orphanage! Someone has to help me find her!'

Rose heard the congregation murmur in disapproval. 'Shame on him, interrupting the Archbishop!'

'Your sister?' The Archbishop sounded completely lost.

Before he could reply, a man burst in at the back of the cathedral and galloped noisily along the aisle. Everyone in the cathedral stared, too shocked to move. The man knocked the boy down. Rose almost leapt to her feet.

'That's for running off, brat!' the man hissed.

Heddsworth's hand went to his rapier. His blue eyes were colder than the winter sky.

'Apologies, apologies, your Grace,' said the strange man, cringing greasily. 'Escaped lunatic – won't 'appen again.'

The boy struggled, landed a punch on the man's jaw, and bolted out of the cathedral. The man angrily rubbed his chin and stormed out after the boy.

The shaken congregation fidgeted with their hymn books. Rose noticed Bronson and Charlie Malone exiting their pew.

'How disgraceful,' muttered Herbert. 'Common riffraff.'

Rose dropped her heavy book of prayer on his foot.

'Ouch!' yelped Herbert.

The congregation shushed him and the Archbishop cleared his throat.

'Does – does anyone else wish to seek pardon?'

Nobody responded. With visible relief, the Archbishop invited everyone to sing a carol.

Rose glanced at Heddsworth. She was desperate to join the other butlers, but they couldn't leave Herbert. Heddsworth drummed his fingers on his hymn book all through *Good King Wenceslas*.

When Rose was almost ready to scream with impatience, the service finally ended, and people began to depart. Emily gave Rose a worried look before leaving with her husband. Herbert was asleep, drooling on his collar. Rose shot to her feet.

'We have to find him, Heddsworth!'

'Bronson and Mr Malone have gone after him,' the butler replied. 'We had best wait until they return first.'

'Was he from an orphanage?' Rose demanded.

'The boy probably escaped from such a place. Very resourceful of him. If his sister is missing from an orphanage, I hope she hasn't been kidnapped by an Angelmaker.'

'What is an Angelmaker?'

Heddsworth's face was pale and set. Only his voice betrayed his anger.

'There are many people who are paid to care for infants and small children. Some are employed privately, some in institutions like orphanages. Most of these people are good, kind-hearted souls who take care of their charges, but not all. If a child dies, there are carers who don't report it and will keep taking the money. The worst deliberately murder their charges. That way they still get paid but don't have the expense of caring for the child.'

'And they're never caught, these Angelmakers?'

'I'm afraid the murders can be hard to prove, Miss Raventhorpe. So many children die of real illnesses.'

As he spoke, Bronson and Charlie Malone entered the nave. Charlie limped heavily, and Bronson looked furious.

'We lost him,' she said, shaking snow off her

clothes. 'I only hope that beast of a man didn't catch him.' She noticed Herbert, who was now snoring. 'Is that your cousin?'

'Yes,' said Rose. 'He expects me to marry him.'

Charlie gave a snort of incredulous laughter.

'It's not going to happen,' said Rose. 'I swear.'

'I should hope not,' said Bronson. 'Well, what are we going to do about the orphan boy and his sister?'

'As the Guardians of Yorke, we should inform the other butlers at Silvercrest Hall,' said Heddsworth.

'We could go there now,' said Rose eagerly. Then she scowled at her snoring cousin. 'I forgot. We have *him* with us.'

'We could leave him in the carriage, I suppose,' mused Heddsworth. 'With a fur rug and some sweets. If he wakes, we'll tell him we're shopping for Christmas presents.'

Rose cheered up. 'What an excellent idea!'

Heddsworth picked Herbert up and carried him

outside. Rose touched the locket she wore on a chain: a cameo carved with a black cat.

She hoped the cat statues were keeping watch on the city. Were they protecting the boy and his missing sister?

Be safe, she thought. *Help is coming.*

Chapter 2

Hall Above, Stairs Below

Rose's heart lifted when she saw Silvercrest Hall. The dignified old building, with its black cat-shaped weather vane, was an academy for butlers of distinction. Few people knew that the butlers also studied fencing and pistol shooting, and helped to keep the city criminals at bay.

They climbed out of the carriage, and the driver took the horse and carriage into the stables, along with a flask of brandy.

Rose and her friends did not go straight indoors.

They were too busy admiring the ice sculptures standing on the front lawn. Two lifesized ice butlers stood frozen, duelling with ice rapiers. There was an ice grandfather clock, complete with ticking pendulum. In one corner reared a beautifully sculpted ice horse and a fierce ice dragon sparkling like polished crystal.

'Who made these?' Rose exclaimed. 'They're the best sculptures I've ever seen!'

'We did,' said Bronson modestly. 'We butlers. It's part of our training.'

Miss Regemont, the imposing head of Hall, met them at the door. She wore a red velvet gown, and a ruby comb in her steel-grey hair.

'Ah, there you are,' she said to the arrivals. 'About time. I need help with arrangements for the Butlers' Ball.'

'*Butlers' Ball*?' said Rose.

'Oh yes, Miss Raventhorpe!' said Heddsworth. 'I was going to tell you about that. We hold a ball every year. You will be invited, I assure you.'

'Me?' said Rose, delighted. 'But I'm not yet old enough to go out in society.'

'Ah, but this is not a regular society ball,' put in Charlie Malone. 'It's quite private – only for the butlers and whoever we decide to invite.'

Rose wondered if Charlie would dance with her. Then she remembered his bad leg.

'I don't go for the dancing,' Charlie added, too heartily. 'I go for the fireworks and the supper.'

Miss Regemont cleared her throat. 'If you haven't come to discuss the ball, then we had better go inside.'

In the ballroom, swags of ivy and holly hung over the fireplace, and a huge Christmas tree glittered with silver baubles. Everyone gathered around a roaring fire. Heddsworth fetched a tray of refreshment, including hot spiced wine, cocoa, and cucumber sandwiches.

'Cucumber sandwiches? In winter?' said Rose.

'Our cucumber sandwiches are a tradition,' said

Miss Regemont firmly. 'I am very particular about them. I once had to expel a student butler for making inferior sandwiches. Now, what brings you here? I gather it is not merely a friendly visit.'

'There was a scene at the Mistletoe Service this morning, Madam,' Heddsworth explained, giving her a full report.

'A missing child,' muttered Miss Regemont. 'From which orphanage?'

'We don't know,' answered Charlie Malone, between sips of cocoa. 'But we can visit them and find out. Most of the orphanages are located around the Muckyards.'

Heddsworth nodded. 'It is our duty as Guardians of the city of Yorke to investigate. I suggest we take the Stairs Below.' He took his pistol from his coat and dusted it off. 'We had better be well armed.'

Charlie Malone drew his rapier and flourished it. 'Sharpeners at the ready!' he crowed.

'What on *earth* is going on here?'

Everyone spun round.

Herbert stood in the doorway, gaping at them all.

'What is this place?' he demanded. 'Rose? Are you consorting with *servants*? Why are they *armed*?'

Rose tried to stay calm. 'Herbert, these are friends of mine. Everyone, this is my cousin Gh— Herbert.'

'Herbert George Ernest Rambleton de Martinet, in line to be the sixth Earl of Dundragan,' corrected her cousin.

'Yes. Well. Herbert, this is Miss Regemont, Charlie Malone, and Bronson.'

Herbert frowned, taking in their uniforms, and the elegant setting of the ballroom. 'Servants?'

'Good evening, Master Herbert,' said Miss Regemont coolly. 'I am the head of this academy. Bronson is a fencing teacher and butler, Mr Malone is a secretary—'

'Butler?' said Herbert, looking Bronson up and down. 'Don't you mean housekeeper?'

The atmosphere in the room dropped ten degrees.

'No,' said Bronson quietly. 'I can serve wine, iron newspapers and manage the staff on an entire estate. I am a butler, *not* a housekeeper.' She drew her rapier. 'And I'll duel the next person who argues with me.'

Heddsworth winced. 'Bronson—'

Herbert turned radish red. 'I knew Heddsworth was useless, but this is ridiculous! This is not fit company for my future wife.'

'I'm not your future wife – I wouldn't marry you if you dragged me to the altar!'

'You should reconsider that, if you want me to keep quiet about *this*,' sneered Herbert, gesturing at the company in the ballroom. 'I heard some talk about Guardians. Your father might have funny modern ideas about acceptable acquaintances, but your mother does not. Butlers wielding weapons – it's revolutionary. It's a threat to the Crown!'

'Master Herbert, there is no need to be upset,' soothed Heddsworth. 'We are simply looking into the matter of some missing children. You can wait in the library while we talk.'

'I will not,' said Herbert. He turned to Rose.

'If you want me to keep quiet about these violent maniacs' – he waved to indicate Bronson's rapier – 'you'd better agree to our engagement. No-one turns down a de Martinet!'

Rose gulped down her outrage. She didn't give a fig about Herbert's pride, but she knew how nasty he could get. If he had Heddsworth sacked, she would be to blame.

'I will consider it.'

Herbert smirked. 'That's better. When we get home, I shall write to inform my father.'

Heddsworth gave Rose a sympathetic glance. She bit her lip. There were more important things to worry about, she told herself. Like the boy from the orphanage. First they would find him, and then she could deal with Ghastly Herbert.

Chapter 3

ORPHEUS OF THE UNDERWORLD

The next day the butlers and Rose took the Stairs Below to the Muckyards.

The Stairs were an underground network of tunnels, with doors that could be unlocked only by the butlers' Infinity Keys. Rose kept one in her cameo necklace. Today, she had told her parents that she was going with Heddsworth to donate old clothes to an orphanage. She hoped they hadn't noticed the long parasol pocket on her coat, which concealed her rapier.

She and her friends walked through the pitch-dark Stairs for a long time, and exited through a doorway in Gigg Street at ten o'clock in the morning. There they entered the drab, crowded streets of the Muckyards. Rose had never set foot in this place before. Here, the buildings leaned together, a precarious collection of paneless windows, warped, hole-ridden roofs, peeling paint and crumbling brick. In their bright, clean clothes, the butlers and Rose attracted suspicious looks from the few people out in the street.

'Don't worry,' said Charlie under his breath. 'I've never had much trouble in this quarter.'

'I doubt you come here often,' Bronson retorted. 'There are not many high teas in the Muckyards.'

They passed a number of dark, narrow tenements, and approached an orphanage.

It was the most forbidding looking building Rose had ever seen. Stone steps led up to stone columns, surmounted by towering stone urns. Neglected trees stood skeletal on either side. The bay windows looked like blind eyes. The roof bore spiky ironwork letters, spelling BLEAKSTONE.

Two men stepped out of an alleyway next to the building, old of eye, rough of knuckle. They stood a few yards from the butlers, grinning, one armed with a knife and one with a cudgel. Rose swallowed hard.

Charlie tipped them a nod. 'Well hello, gentlemen. Pleasant day for a stroll, isn't it?'

They stared at him. '"Pleasant day"?' one mimicked. 'Ooh, there's fancy talk.'

'May we pass?' Charlie added. 'It's just that you're in our way.'

One thug stepped closer. 'Empty your pockets, you lot,' he growled. 'Or we'll cut yer to ribbons.'

'Oh, very well,' sighed Bronson, unsheathing her rapier.

One of the ruffians darted forward at her with his knife. Bronson pivoted and lunged. Her attacker reeled back with a curse. 'Get the cripple, Nabber!' he yelled.

Nabber threw himself towards Charlie Malone just as Charlie drew his blade and swept it out in an arc. Nabber howled, clutching his belly. He kicked Charlie's bad leg. Charlie dropped, rolled, and whipped the blade up to the man's throat. Slowly, Nabber backed away.

The first ruffian was now trying to stab Heddsworth. He managed to cut Heddsworth's arm before the butler deftly ducked under Bronson's blade, and kicked the knife from his attacker's hand. Rose, shocked to see Heddsworth injured, rashly ran towards him. Then both ruffians dived towards Rose.

Bronson had trained Rose remorselessly for hours, and Rose acted instinctively. A swipe of the blade at one ruffian's legs made him jerk backwards, and a swift two-handed strike knocked the knife from his grip. Nabber took aim with his cudgel, but the butlers gave him no chance to use it. All three pointed their rapiers at his throat.

Cursing, both men fled.

Rose wiped her sweaty hands on her coat.

Bronson began cleaning her rapier with a handkerchief. 'Well done, everyone. Heddsworth, did you bring any supplies?'

'A flask of hot tea,' said Heddsworth. 'I have a light flesh wound to deal with. Mr Malone, a bandage?'

Charlie immediately checked Heddsworth's bleeding arm. 'Hmm, you're lucky that was no deeper. Bronson, keep watch while I deal with this, will you?'

'Gladly,' said Bronson, sheathing her blade and standing guard.

'Miss Raventhorpe,' said Heddsworth, 'Go to the orphanage.'

Rose sheathed her own rapier. Then she sped up the stone steps and thumped the iron knocker.

The grimy brass doorknob turned. A pair of alert green eyes appeared in the doorway. They belonged to a girl of about eight, whose brown hair was curled so tightly she looked like a cocklebur.

'Has you come to buy an orphan?' she whispered.

'Pardon me?' asked Rose.

'Cause the master charges very high, Miss.'

'Er, I'd like to see the master, please.'

The girl opened the door further. 'Come in.'

Rose followed her down a passageway. She glanced into the doorways of rooms where children huddled in groups. Some cried, or whispered, but none seemed to be playing. Some looked sickly, and Rose wondered who was taking care of them. The whole atmosphere was cold and miserable.

'What's your name?' she asked the girl.

'Smith, Miss.'

'I mean your first name.'

'Oh. Corrie, Miss.'

'I'm Rose. How long have you lived here, Corrie?'

'Since I was three, Miss.'

'How are you treated?'

'Like it's Christmas every day,' recited the girl dully, as if it was a lesson drummed into her.

Rose whispered to Corrie. 'Do you know of a runaway boy? He had a sister who might have stayed here.'

'Orpheus? He was sent to the mill months ago, but he came back for Inaaya,' whispered Corrie. 'But we don't know where she's gone.'

'When did you see her last?'

Corrie frowned, thinking. 'Not long.'

'How many days?' Rose prompted.

'About twelve,' said Corrie, counting on her fingers. 'Orpheus came looking for her the day before yesterday. Cornpepper shouted at him, and he had to run.'

'Where did you last see Inaaya?'

'Her bed, in the dormitory.' Corrie led Rose into a long, cold room, lined with a dozen beds. The orphan girl pointed one out. 'She slept there.'

Rose walked over to the bed, wondering if Inaaya had left any clue here of her disappearance. If she had been kidnapped, would there be signs of a struggle? Rose ran her hand over the thin blanket, and lifted the pillow. Nothing. Then she tried the mattress. It was hard, and smelled like musty straw. Something caught Rose's eye, up in the furthest corner. A folded piece of paper. She reached for it, unfolding it gingerly.

It was a charcoal drawing. It looked like a bird with sprawling, raggedy wings, and had obviously been sketched in a hurry. Rose frowned. 'What is this?'

'I don't know,' whispered Corrie, looking perplexed. 'Inaaya couldn't write many words, but she liked to draw. Maybe it was a message for Orpheus.'

Rose heard footsteps at the doorway and the growl of a dog. She shoved the paper into her pocket. Corrie grabbed Rose's hand as both girls turned to face the doorway.

'Ahh, shut up, Lucifer,' snapped a voice. A man entered the room with a black mastiff padding at his side. Rose recognised him at once. Tall, thin and weak-chinned, he was the one who had seized

Orpheus at the cathedral and chased him away. His face was disfigured by the scars of smallpox.

The man scowled at Rose. 'Who are you? What d'you want? It's trespassin', bein' in here without my sayso.'

Rose cleared her throat.

'Good morning, sir. I'm searching for an orphan who might do as a servant,' she said, in her best ladylike manner. 'I take it you are the master here?'

'I'm Jabez Cornpepper.' He scratched at his ear. 'I run the place. What kind of orphan you want? That 'un there, that girl, she's worth four shillin'.'

Corrie glanced nervously at Rose.

'Are you the owner of Bleakstone, Mr Cornpepper?'

'Nope, I just manages the place. Four shillin' is reasonable for an orphan.'

'Well,' said Rose. 'As it happens, I am looking for a boy of about thirteen. Do you have one?'

'Thirteen?' said Cornpepper. 'We don't usually

keep 'em that long. Send 'em out to be apprentices and such. We only 'ad one boy that old.'

'May I see him then?'

'No,' Cornpepper retorted. 'He's gone, an' good riddance too.'

'Oh,' said Rose. 'How unfortunate. Do you have any girls close to that age then? Perhaps the boy had a sister? A girl would do just as well.'

'He did, as it happens, but she's run off.'

Corrie made a tiny, startled noise.

'Not that he believed it, the little brat,' Cornpepper added.

'I imagine he was upset,' said Rose, stiff-lipped with fury.

'Dunno why,' said Cornpepper. 'Family's just a nuisance. I should know. Got a sister of me own.'

'How sad for her,' muttered Rose. 'Why did the girl run away, sir?'

'How would I know? She was only a foreigner's brat. They're all ungrateful for a roof over their heads,' he replied, with a shrug.

'She said the food was bad,' whispered Corrie.

'Enough of that,' warned Cornpepper, and the dog growled.

'Who does own this place?' Rose wanted to know.

'Not me,' said Cornpepper irritably. 'There's a committee that I reports to. I takes me orders from them, and they don't interfere as long as I does me job. Which I do. And I don't like snoops and funny questions, Miss. We don't get many fancy sorts in the Muckyards.'

'I happen to think orphans should be put to good use,' said Rose, in her haughtiest tone. 'And I have servants to protect me in this unfortunate district.'

'Well, if you ain't about to buy an orphan, Miss Whoever-You-Are, you'd better be goin'. I've got me nose to the grindstone.'

'Very well,' said Rose with a sigh. 'If I must. I cannot see any orphans here that are suitable.'

She gave Corrie an apologetic nod. She wished

she could take every orphan away from this place. But Cornpepper was still staring at her through narrowed eyes. She let him slam the door behind her, and went to see how the butlers were faring.

Charlie Malone was tying off a bandage on Heddsworth's arm. Bronson stood on guard with her rapier. There were no ruffians in sight.

'Quite a good fight,' Heddsworth was saying. 'Though now I shall have to repair this coat.' He turned to Rose. 'Ah, Miss Raventhorpe! How did it go?'

Rose was about to explain when there was a sudden interruption. A figure stepped out from behind a stairway. It was the boy from the cathedral, Orpheus, and his eyes were fierce with fear and rage and determination. He held a small stub of a knife.

'Where's my sister?' he hissed. 'Did you steal her?'

'Orpheus!' Rose rushed towards him. 'We're friends! We want to help you.'

The boy glanced rapidly from Rose to the others. The butlers sheathed their weapons.

'We saw you in the cathedral,' said Rose. 'We know your sister is missing.'

'How do you know my name?'

'I – I asked the orphans,' Rose began.

The boy kicked her in the shin.

'Ouch! I'm trying to help you, Orpheus!'

Charlie Malone gripped the boy by the shoulders. 'It's all right,' he said. 'Please, listen. We're not going to hurt you. Put that knife away. We're not Angelmakers.'

'Who are you then?'

Rose rubbed her shin. 'I'm Rose Raventhorpe, and this is Heddsworth, Bronson and Charlie Malone. They are butlers who like to duel. With swords.'

The boy put a hand to his wild hair. 'Butlers?' he said incredulously. 'But who do you all work for?'

'Not for childstealers,' said Rose. 'Look, this isn't the best place for explanations.'

'Quite right. We'll take young Orpheus, is it? – to Miss Raventhorpe's home,' said Heddsworth. 'Here, take my coat, lad. You must be freezing.'

The boy still looked suspicious but he replaced the small blade in his pocket and put on Heddsworth's coat.

'Oh come along,' Rose said crossly. 'I don't want you dragged back into that orphanage.'

Lucifer barked distantly inside. The boy flinched. 'Fine,' he muttered. 'But don't think I'm stupid.'

They ushered him down to Gigg Street. Heddsworth hailed a hansom cab. 'Will you be all right taking Orpheus home?' he asked Rose. 'I had better report to Miss Regemont.'

'Of course,' said Rose. 'We'll see you back at Lambsgate.'

She and Orpheus climbed into the cab, Heddsworth gave orders to the driver, and they set off. Orpheus sat in the furthest corner from Rose, as if ready to leap out of the window.

'Are you rich or something?' he asked her.

'Well yes, my family is,' Rose admitted.

'Why do you have a sword? In fact ... Why do you all have swords?'

41

Rose hesitated. 'They need protection in a place like the Muckyards,' she said at last.

Orpheus snorted. 'They don't act like people who need protection. They're not like any servants I've seen in England. They're more like bodyguards, or soldiers.'

'Yes. They *are* like that,' said Rose slowly. 'I suppose if you are going to trust us, you should know the truth.' She took a deep breath. 'They are a secret society – the Guardians of Yorke. As for me, well, the Raventhorpes have always been the city's protectors.'

Orpheus shook his head, as if bemused. 'Guardians,' he muttered.

Rose paused. 'What's your last name?'

'Rayburn.'

'And you used to live in the orphanage with your sister? What happened to your parents?'

Orpheus sighed. 'Our pa was an English sailor, and our mother was from Delhi. They're both dead. That's how me and Inaaya ended up in Bleakstone.

We spent two years in that hole.' He spat out the window.

'I'm sorry about your family,' said Rose softly. 'We want to help find your sister. We saw you in the cathedral. You were really brave.'

Orpheus winced. 'I was scared witless.'

'Have you lived in Yorke all your life?'

'No. We used to sail with our pa. He got shore leave because Inaaya was sick. But he ended up sick himself . . . and he died.' Orpheus swallowed. 'We got put in Bleakstone. Inaaya recovered but Cornpepper said I was too much trouble, and sold me to a mill owner in Bagford. That was almost worse than Bleakstone. I ran away a few days ago and came to get Inaaya but she'd disappeared. If I'd only come a few weeks earlier . . . '

'What happened, exactly?'

'I don't know. I asked Cornpepper where she was and he told me and the others that she'd run away. It's all a lie! He'd be raving if anyone really escaped Bleakstone! He wouldn't answer any of my questions, just tried to grab me and lock me up again. So I had to run. I don't know if he's sold her to another mill owner, or – or worse. But she'd never go anywhere without me if she had a choice. She knew I was coming back for her.'

Rose took the piece of paper from her pocket. 'I found this under her mattress. Is it Inaaya's?'

Orpheus unfolded it. 'Yes,' he said, biting his lip. 'It must be meant for me. But what is it?'

'A crow?' Rose guessed. 'The bodysnatchers? It wouldn't surprise me if *they* stole children.'

The boy lifted his eyebrows. 'Bodysnatchers?'

'People who dig up corpses for money,' Rose explained. 'For anatomists to cut up for science. But then, the Crows are in prison, the ones I know about,' she mused. 'So she must mean some other kind of bird.'

'Maybe,' said Orpheus. 'Inaaya's only six. She can't write very well, so she had to draw something.'

'It could be a raven. There's a street in Yorke named Ravensgate,' said Rose. 'And I'm a

Raventhorpe. But I doubt your sister was referring to us.'

Orpheus folded the paper up carefully and tucked it away in his shirt. 'I'll find out what she meant. And if she's alive, I'm going to find her.'

'We will,' said Rose. 'We want to help.'

The cab turned into the Shudders, the narrow street filled with Yorke's finest shops and taverns.

Orpheus gasped, and pointed out the window. 'There's a bird! Right there!'

Rose leaned over his shoulder and looked outside. A fierce-eyed crow was perched behind a glass window only a few feet away, and it was staring right back at her.

Chapter 4

Buttercrumbe's Curiosities

'Stop here, please!'

The driver obeyed. Rose and Orpheus climbed out. 'Wait for us,' Rose instructed the driver.

They went to the shop window and peered up at the crow.

It wasn't alive. It was part of a display at a taxidermist's called Buttercrumbe's Curiosities. Rose had heard of Buttercrumbe's talent. People came from miles around to see his eerily lifelike creatures. The window display was of kittens having a tea party, while the crow sat above them with a cup of tea in his claws. A sign read 'Mrs Whiskers Entertains Her Guests'. The whole shop was full of amazing yet disgusting things. Rose saw a stuffed polar bear, giraffe skeletons, a giant crab in an aquarium and a very dead dodo. Further back in the shop was a skeleton labelled as a 'Hawaiian mer-lady' and a stuffed two-headed lamb.

Orpheus was baffled. 'Why would anyone dress up dead kittens?'

'I think it's meant to be funny,' said Rose.

She pushed open the door, which set off a jingling bell. A tall man looked at them from behind a counter. Fluffy grey hair framed his balding head. His forehead was as precisely lined as a music score and his nose was long enough for a bird to perch on. Rose smelled glue and feathers.

'Good morning,' he said amiably. 'I'm Mr Buttercrumbe. Are you here for something in particular?'

'Not quite,' said Rose. 'May we look around your shop?'

'Certainly, but be sure not to touch anything. I work to preserve the rare, you see, and the beautiful. Some creatures must be recreated for museums. Terrible, you know, how some species are dying out. I always dream of working with dinosaur bones, but it is a disadvantage not having the skin to work with.' Mr Buttercrumbe gazed lovingly at his 'creatures'.

'Ah, yes,' said Rose.

'Did you kill these animals, then?' asked Orpheus.

'No!' said Mr Buttercrumbe, in a shocked tone. 'I only preserve noble creatures when they have reached the end of their natural lives.' He gave Rose a card. It read, 'Bramley Buttercrumbe's Curiosities. Precious Animals Preserved for Posterity.'

Rose pointed to the bird in the window. 'Is that a crow?'

'Yes – fine example of the bird. Reasonable price if you are buying!'

'Perhaps another time,' said Rose. 'Mr Buttercrumbe, we are looking for a lost girl, about six years old. Orpheus's sister. Have you seen any lost children?'

'I do not let many children in here,' said Mr Buttercrumbe apologetically. 'They touch the displays. Make silly jokes. Bring in gnats and dead flies, and say I should preserve them.'

'Do you have children yourself?' inquired Rose.

'No,' sighed Buttercrumbe. 'If you hear of any young folk interested in apprenticing to my trade, let me know.'

The door opened, and a man edged into the shop. His drooping moustache, pasty complexion and fraying clothes gave him a shifty appearance.

'Ah,' said Buttercrumbe. 'Flinty. How may I help you today?'

'I've come on hard times, sir,' Flinty said, turning his hat in his hands. 'Hate to part with anything of value, but it's meant to be preserved for the ages, isn't it?' He put a hand in his pocket and revealed a small grey arrowhead.

Buttercrumbe inspected the arrowhead. He sighed.

'You are a master of your craft, sir. I only wish you could find the honest way to use it.'

'But I am honest, sir!' cried Flinty, in injured tones. 'It's a genuine rock! Made back in the old times.'

'Dear sir, this was not created by a caveman. My underwear is older than this arrowhead. I know newborn fleas with longer life spans! If this is a genuine article, Flinty, I will eat my moustache wax.'

'You're a hard man to please,' sighed Flinty.

'Sorry,' said the older man gently. As Flinty moved away, Buttercrumbe whispered to Rose and Orpheus. 'Flinty the Fox. Otherwise known as Flinty the Forger. Very good at crafting fake antiquities.'

'It's only 'cause I can't find enough real ones,' said Flinty indignantly. He crossed his arms. 'It's unfair, that's what it is. At this rate I'll have to start workin' as a Raven.'

Rose and Orpheus started.

'What ravens?' asked Orpheus.

'Chimney sweeps,' said Flinty. 'The Raven Society, they calls themselves.'

'Oh,' said Rose. 'I see.'

Orpheus stared at him suspiciously.

Flinty studied her hopefully. 'Are you interested in buying a nice antique rock collection?'

'No she isn't!' said Buttercrumbe. He glared at Flinty. 'Off you go now. You are not to bother my customers.'

Sulkily, Flinty left the shop.

Rose smiled at Mr Buttercrumbe. 'Thank you for letting us look around.'

'You are welcome,' he replied while carefully stretching out a bat's wing.

Rose and Orpheus hurried out the door.

'There's something not right about that place!' gasped Orpheus.

'It's a little strange,' conceded Rose. 'But at least we learned something. We'll have to look into the matter of the Ravens. Perhaps that was what your sister was trying to draw. A raven, for a sweep.'

'A sweep,' mused Orpheus. For the first time he looked at Rose as if he trusted her. 'Cornpepper used to threaten to sell us to the sweeps. Maybe that's what happened to Inaaya. It's definitely a start.'

Back at Lambsgate, just after lunchtime, Rose smuggled Orpheus into the kitchen via the servants' entrance. As soon as he sat down, Watchful the cat jumped into his lap. Orpheus, leaning tiredly back in his chair, smiled and let the cat sniff at his fingers.

Heddsworth had stopped on the way home to buy Orpheus some new clothes. There was a shirt, trousers, boots, a flared tailcoat and a tricorn hat. Once he'd had a wash and changed in the servants' bathroom, the combined effect was dashing. He had a nap in the chair while Rose told Heddsworth about their experiences at Buttercrumbe's.

Mrs Standish the cook, shocked by the boy's

half-starved appearance, served him rice pudding, followed by vegetable soup, then strawberry tarts with whipped cream. Orpheus stared at each serving as if his wildest dreams were coming true.

Mrs Standish patted the boy's cheek. 'Dreadful places, them orphanages. Hate to think what they fed you.'

'Cabbage custard, mostly,' said Orpheus. 'And some other awful green gloop.'

'Disgusting,' said Mrs Standish feelingly. 'Well, I'd better go see M'Lady about tonight's dinner menu.' She bustled out.

'I will tell his Lordship we need a new boy on the house staff,' said Heddsworth. 'Would that suit you, Master Orpheus?'

'You want to employ me?' Orpheus gaped at him.

'Certainly,' said Heddsworth. 'We will provide bed and board, and a salary.'

Bixby entered the kitchen. 'What is going on here?' he asked, in disdain. 'Are we serving tea to guests in the servants' quarters now?'

'New member of staff,' said Heddsworth. 'His name is Orpheus.'

'Dear me,' sniffed Bixby. 'I shall add him to my long list of things to remove from the house. Once you are sacked of course, Mr Heddsworth.'

Everyone looked at him with loathing.

Bixby eyed Rose. 'Eating with the staff, Miss Raventhorpe? Master Herbert will be most disapproving.' And he swanned out.

Heddsworth drew a long breath.

'I hope we can find your missing sister, young man. Perhaps that picture does refer to the Raven Society. If so, we shall have to speak to them, and that will be difficult.'

'Why is that?' Rose inquired.

'I'm afraid we Silvercrest butlers don't get on with them.'

'You don't like the chimney sweeps? Why ever not?' asked Rose.

'Oh, we used to be allies,' said Heddsworth. 'We butlers need to know trustworthy chimney sweeps to work for our employers. If the Society had news for us – such as reports of criminal activity that the Guardians might stop – they dropped messages down our kitchen chimneys. And if they needed help, we did our best to provide it.

'But that was a few years ago. Rumours spread of the sweeps stealing orphan children to work as their apprentices. It is true the sweeps used to employ children, but I don't believe they were stolen. However, that rumour was enough to spoil our alliance. The Society stopped communicating with us. They stick to their meeting place, the Ravens' Nest, in the Muckyards. The practice of employing children is outlawed now, but there is still bad feeling between the butlers and the Ravens.'

'I'm not sure Inaaya was kidnapped,' said Rose. 'She had time to leave that picture.'

'I think she meant to send me a message,' said Orpheus. 'She would do that, if we weren't allowed to talk to each other at the orphanage.'

Heddsworth drummed his fingers on the table.

'We should follow up the matter. We shall have to discuss this at Silvercrest Hall. But first I shall send word to the Raven Society. Hopefully they will agree to talk.'

They went to Silvercrest Hall the next day. Orpheus raised his eyebrows at the grand establishment, with its handsome staircase and display case of ancient swords.

Miss Regemont invited them into her office where Bronson and Charlie Malone were waiting. A fire burned in the hearth, and tea steamed in a silver pot. The butlers inspected Inaaya's sketch.

'Do we know anyone with a birdlike name?' asked Charlie Malone. 'Apart from Miss Raventhorpe?'

'There's a butler named Byrd who works in Vicarsgate,' mused Bronson. 'But I hardly think he's worth worrying about. That's the only surname I know of. I don't even know the first names of some of the butlers in Yorke.'

Charlie Malone grinned suddenly. 'Some people hate their first names. Do you know Heddsworth's, Miss Raventhorpe?'

Rose's eyes widened. 'No. What is it?'

'It is hardly of consequence, Miss Raventhorpe.'

'Can't you tell us?' coaxed Charlie. 'I'm curious, now.'

Heddsworth's face reddened. 'I prefer to go by my middle name, which is James.'

'But what's the real one?' persisted Rose. 'At least the first initial.'

'I know,' said Bronson. 'It starts with A.'

'A?' said Rose. 'Andrew? Augustus?'

'Amaryllis?' suggested Charlie.

'Oh, stop this,' snapped Miss Regemont. 'We are dealing with the matter of a missing child.'

Rose glanced down, embarrassed. The others cast apologetic looks at Orpheus.

'It's all right,' said Orpheus. 'I'm glad that you're all willing to hel—'

Something rattled in the chimney, making

everyone jump. Then a choking pile of soot and ash tumbled into the fireplace.

'What the—' began Bronson.

Heddsworth shot to his feet. 'I believe a trip to the rooftop is necessary, Miss Regemont. The Raven Society will be waiting.'

Rose, Orpheus and the butlers followed Heddsworth up several flights of stairs. Eventually they reached an attic, crowded with trunks of cutlery and empty old wine bottles. Heddsworth opened a skylight, letting in a blast of wintry air. 'We put this in the roof some years ago,' he explained to Rose. 'When we were still friends with the sweeps.' Then he climbed out on to the roof, helping the others out after him.

It was piercingly cold. The wind howled. Rose gritted her teeth. Then she saw a stranger on the rooftop.

He looked like a woebegone beggar, with watery sad eyes and a greying beard. His top hat and tailcoat would have suited an undertaker. A tame raven sat on his shoulder. In one hand he held a sack, which must have contained the soot and ash he had poured down the chimney. A fireplace poker lay at his feet.

'Hello sir,' said Heddsworth.

'You sent a message,' rasped the man. 'I'm Fawney, leader of the Raven Society.' He glanced at the children. 'Who are the bairns?'

'My young employer Miss Raventhorpe and her friend Orpheus. You are welcome to come indoors if you wish.'

'Not goin' into the Hall,' said Fawney stubbornly. He patted one of the chimneys. 'This 'un's warm. Stand up here.'

They all went to the chimney, and leaned gratefully against the warm bricks.

'I contacted you because a child is missing,' said Heddsworth. 'A little girl, an orphan.'

Fawney grunted. 'And you think we've stolen 'er? That'd be you butlers all over.'

'She's my sister!' Orpheus blurted out. 'Do the Ravens know anything about her?'

59

The sweep scowled, and the raven flapped its wings angrily.

'No, and I'm not helpin' nobody,' Fawney shot back. 'I'm 'ere to warn you lot to stay out of our affairs. We won't 'ave no nosin' about.'

'I assure you, Fawney, we are not nosing,' said Miss Regemont crossly. 'We only wish to find a missing child.'

'Well we ain't seen no missin' child. We ain't stolen any either, no matter what you lot think. Understand?' Fawney picked up the fireplace poker.

Heddsworth sighed. 'I'm not armed, Fawney. I don't wish to fight.'

'Things 'as changed then,' said Fawney, scowling. 'You butlers like wavin' swords too much if you ask me.'

Despite the warmth of the chimney, Rose's feet were numb. She could barely feel her fingers. Orpheus was shivering, his jaw clenched to still his chattering teeth.

'If you do hear of a lost girl,' said Rose, 'please tell us.'

'We won't,' said Fawney, and turned away. With great dexterity he began to climb down a drainpipe. The raven flapped its wings and circled in the ice-grey sky.

Chapter 5

THE RAVENS' NEST

Rose woke up the next day determined to carry on with their investigation. The unhelpful Fawney had been a disappointment, but she was not ready to give up.

'*We* can talk to him,' she told Orpheus in the kitchen. 'He mightn't talk to the butlers, but we aren't from Silvercrest Hall. Maybe if we go to the Ravens' Nest—'

She stopped. Herbert had entered the room.

'Still in the kitchen, Rose?' he drawled. 'Really, I

won't have this. I will have to speak to your mother. Unless . . . '

'What do you want?' snapped Rose.

'I have decided we should take the carriage for a special outing. Dreadful weather, but that is what one must expect in this horrid northern climate.' He looked down his nose at Orpheus, who was polishing silver. 'Mind you don't pocket any of that, kitchen boy.'

Rose almost threw the tin of silver polish at her cousin.

'Where do you plan to take me?' she asked, with an effort.

'It's a secret,' said Herbert. 'You'll see when we get there.'

'It would be improper to go alone,' said Rose sharply. 'I'd like Orpheus to come with us. He can help Jeremiah to drive the carriage.'

'If he must,' sighed Herbert. 'Probably best to keep him out of temptation's way. He'll be idle otherwise.'

Just then, Watchful the cat bit Herbert on the ankle.

Orpheus whisked the cat out of the kitchen while Herbert hopped about, swearing. When he returned, he shared a secret smile with Rose. 'I gave Watchful a whole haddock,' he whispered to her. 'He deserves it.'

To Rose's surprise, Herbert took her to Locks and Clocks.

The well-established shop was run by the Goldsmith family and offered exquisitely designed clocks and jewellery. It had grandfather clocks which not only showed astronomical conjunctions but comets and falling stars. Orpheus helped the driver to blanket the horses, while Rose entered the shop with Herbert.

Rose looked around for Miss Garnet Goldsmith but saw only her pretty sister, Sapphire.

'How may I help you?' Sapphire inquired. She looked unusually strained, not her usual charming self.

'I require an engagement ring,' answered Herbert.

Rose's head swivelled towards him. 'What?'

'Our engagement ring, of course,' said Herbert condescendingly. 'You needn't wear it yet. But it is only proper that I should choose you a ring. I hope you'll be properly grateful.'

Rose felt like a boiling tea kettle. 'I am *not* marrying you!'

'Do stop being tiresome, Rose,' sighed Herbert. 'I thought you'd be pleased, going to this poky little place instead of a proper London establishment.'

Sapphire watched this exchange nervously. 'Perhaps you might like to look at our diamond rings?' she suggested. 'With ruby and emerald, for a Christmas engagement?'

'Yes, that might do,' said Herbert, picking up a ring to inspect it.

Rose looked at Sapphire. 'How is Garnet? I was hoping to talk to her.'

Sapphire paled. 'Oh – she's unwell today. I'm sure she would be happy to help you another time.'

'I'm sorry to hear that,' said Rose. Garnet was a talented jeweller, although she was not allowed to officially work as one. She had made the cameo locket that Rose wore constantly on a necklace.

As Mr Goldsmith emerged from his workshop, Rose was startled by his haggard appearance. He usually had a smile, full of gold teeth, for her. Now he was rubbing at dark circles under his eyes.

'Miss Raventhorpe! A pleasure to see you.'

'Thank you,' said Rose. 'I'm sorry to hear Garnet is unwell.'

'Yes,' said Mr Goldsmith. 'An unpleasant cold, poor child. But she'll be back at work soon. I need her help.' His fingers trembled a little as he rested them on the bench. 'Mr Heddsworth is not with you today?'

'No, I'm here with my cousin. Is everything all right, Mr Goldsmith?'

'Oh yes. Quite.' He picked up a diamond bracelet, and put it down again.

Rose turned back to Herbert. 'This is all rather

exhausting,' she said, with sudden sweetness. 'You choose a ring, Herbert, and I'll go shopping. I'll have Orpheus carry my packages. I can take a hansom cab home. I'm sure you don't need me to help you.'

Herbert looked suspicious, but Sapphire quickly turned to him. 'Let's see if we can find something fine enough for you, sir.'

'Oh, all right then,' Herbert said, with a shrug.

Rose bolted outside.

'Jeremiah, you may wait for Master Herbert,' she told the surprised driver. 'Orpheus is coming for a walk with me.'

'Ye're sure, Miss?'

'Yes, thank you. We will be fine.'

She led a puzzled Orpheus away along the street. 'Orpheus,' she hissed, 'do you know where the Ravens' Nest is? The place Miss Regemont spoke of?'

'I reckon so,' he whispered back. 'Saw the place before we ended up in Bleakstone. It's in the Muckyards. Why?'

'Because we're going to go there and talk to Fawney.'

'Better change our clothes,' Orpheus warned. 'We can't walk into the Nest looking like toffs.'

'Oh bother,' said Rose. 'You're right. We shall have to buy a few things.'

They found a shop which sold second-hand clothing and outfitted themselves. Rose replaced her flower-trimmed hat with an old servant's cap, and covered her dress with a moth-eaten gown that smelled like rotting vegetables.

'We'll take the Stairs Below,' she told Orpheus. 'I don't know all the doors yet, but I know the nearest one to the Shudders.'

As they walked, she explained about the secret passageways under the city. Only the butlers of Yorke could access them, using Infinity Keys. Rose, as an honorary Guardian, was the one exception. Her own key was hidden in her cameo locket, and she never felt right without it around her neck.

When she spotted the right door, she checked that nobody was watching before she opened it with her key.

They descended several steps into the cool darkness. Orpheus took one of the lanterns waiting just inside, and lit it using the matches Rose always kept in her pocket.

'Are you sure you know where to go, Rose?'

'I hope so. If we lose our sense of direction, we can open a door, and check where we are. There are doors all over the city, so it's not hard to find one. We just have to stick to safe paths. Heddsworth has marked the unsafe ones with an X.'

'What do we say if we meet a butler down here?'

'We shall tell them we are on a special mission,' said Rose. *What would Heddsworth say if he knew her plan?* She hoped he wouldn't find out.

They set off northwards, through the dark tunnels. Rose counted the doors they passed, mindful of the oil level in the lantern. At last she stopped at one, and took out her key.

'Ready?' she asked Orpheus.

He nodded.

Rose turned the key in the lock. The door opened, and Orpheus extinguished the lantern.

They stepped out into the top of Gigg Street. The traffic was noisy, with carts and wagons and people struggling doggedly through the snow. Orpheus pulled his hat low over his face and Rose did the same with her cap. 'Right,' she said. 'The Ravens' Nest. Lead the way.'

As they trudged off in the same direction as Bleakstone Orphanage, the streets grew shabbier and dirtier. Squalid. Rats feasted on a muck pile. A couple shouted at each other in the street, using language so fiery it practically singed Rose's ears.

'It's down this skitterway,' said Orpheus.

A sign swung outside the building, crudely painted with a raven on its nest. Everything, from the door to the windows, roof and floors, was tilted askew.

The two children pushed at the door. Something was blocking the way. They shoved harder and this time the door squeaked open. There was a harsh cawing, and Rose started as a bird flapped out of a cage by the door. She nearly tripped over a man lying across the floor in front of them.

'Ah, leave 'im,' said a woman's voice. 'The old sod blocks the draughts.'

They stepped gingerly over the man who reeked of whisky fumes. Rose looked about. The place was dark, dingy, and scattered with feathers and bird droppings. Customers stared warily at Rose and Orpheus.

Rose spotted Fawney, drinking at a table. Before she could say anything the woman at the bar, a black-haired creature in a greasy apron, held up a bloody carving knife.

'You two brought me my birds?'

'Birds?' said Rose faintly.

'Aye,' said the woman. 'For me bird pie. Delivery's late.'

'We're not delivery people, I'm sorry,' said Rose. 'What is bird pie? Do you mean fowl?'

'"Foul"?' screeched the woman. 'I'll give you "foul"! I use good game for me pies. Pheasants, quail, bits of pigeon.'

'Sounds delicious,' said Orpheus hastily. 'Can't wait to try it.'

She looked appeased. 'Pay your brass and I'll cut you a slice.'

Rose handed over some coins. 'What was your name, Ma'am?'

'Mrs Mollisher,' grunted the woman. 'And don't sweet-talk me, it's still twopence.'

Orpheus handed the plate to Rose. The pie was all beaks, bones and claws. The pastry was gristle and glue.

She carried the horrid dish up to Fawney's table. 'Can we sit here?'

'If ye must,' grunted Fawney. His pet raven eyed Rose malevolently. She wished she had Watchful with her.

'Do you remember us?' she whispered.

He looked at them more closely. Then he nearly

choked on his ale. 'You're the young 'uns that was on the roof!'

'I'm Rose,' she told him, 'and this is Orpheus. We know you don't like the butlers, and I'm sorry, but we're hoping you can help us. We need to know if the sweeps have anything to do with Orpheus's missing sister.'

Fawney glared at them. Then he went to the meagre fire that burned in the fireplace. He crouched on the hearth and drew his fingers through the ashes.

Orpheus followed him. 'What are you doing?'

'I'm askin' the ashes a question, boy.'

The sweep drew several lines in the ashes, muttering to himself. Then he sat back on his haunches and waited. The fire flickered and a draught whooshed down the chimney.

Fawney scrutinised the ashes again and came back over to the table. 'They say you're to be helped,' he said, grudgingly.

Rose had never expected to feel grateful to ashes.

'Well,' she said. 'Good. So is there any chance you have seen a six-year-old girl? Tell him what she looks like, Orpheus.'

'Black hair like mine, cut short. Brown skin, about this tall,' said Orpheus, holding his hand out at chest height. She vanished from Bleakstone Orphanage about twelve days ago.'

Fawney sat heavily down. 'Haven't seen anyone like that, but I can send word around. What other questions you got?'

Orpheus showed him Inaaya's sketch. 'My sister drew this before she was taken. I thought it might be a raven.'

The sweep narrowed his gaze. 'Could be. Could be any sort of bird.'

'Well, yes,' said Rose. 'But even if it wasn't anything to do with the Raven Society,' she explained tactfully, 'you chimney sweeps must travel around the city and visit a good many houses. We thought you might know something.'

Fawney sat in thought for a moment. Then he

returned to the ashes, and scraped through them with the poker. 'Wood,' he said at last. 'The ashes say you should talk to Angus Wood. He's workin' at the Highborne today. A good sweep, knows his job.'

'The ashes say we should talk to Wood?' Orpheus scratched his head.

'Aye,' said Fawney, brows lowering. 'Summat wrong wi' that?'

'No. My pa was a sailor, and sailors are very supersti—we believe in signs and things,' said Orpheus.

'We shall go to the Highborne,' Rose promised Fawney. 'Thank you for talking to us.'

The sweep paused. 'Wait. If we're to be talkin', like, you needs to know our signs. Where is it you live? Lambsgate? I can drop a message down the chimney if I needs to.'

'Really?' said Rose, intrigued.

'Aye. If we can't get to the chimney, we gets our ravens to send messages. If you sees my bird on your window ledge, you opens it and check 'is leg.'

'I'll remember,' said Rose. 'What kind of message would you send?'

Fawney reached into a pocket, and brought out a handful of odds and ends. He laid them out on the table. A rusty nail. The handle from a china cup. An old brass key.

'The cup handle means "We want a meeting". As in, we need to talk,' he explained. 'The key means "We know summat useful". And the nail means "Danger", "Watch out", that kinda thing. Got it?'

Rose and Orpheus nodded.

'Keep an eye on yer fireplaces,' he said, sweeping the items back into his pocket. 'And we'll see if we can find this missing girl.'

The Highborne Hotel was a long way from the Muckyards. Rose and Orpheus changed their clothes again and Rose hailed a hansom cab.

When they arrived they entered through large

revolving doors. The ceiling was painted with images of fat cherubs atop white clouds. An orchestra was playing Christmas carols and teacups clinked daintily in the dining room. The children could smell roast beef and mince pies. Their stomachs growled almost in unison – it was nearly lunchtime.

A tall, middle-aged man in butler livery approached them. He had a receding hairline, a superior expression, and the regal air of someone who actually owned the hotel, rather than merely working in it. His lapel sported a golden peacock pin.

'It's Mr Mayfair,' whispered Rose. 'The hotel butler.'

'Ah, Miss Raventhorpe,' said Mayfair, with a bow. 'A pleasure to see you.'

'Thank you. Mayfair, this is Orpheus Rayburn.'

Orpheus swept his hat from his head.

'The hotel is looking very fine.'

'Oh yes,' said Mayfair proudly. 'Do you like the

Christmas decorations? We spent weeks choosing and arranging them. All our cutlery has received a special polish. And we have a splendid array of treasures on loan from the Yorke Museum. A fine Renaissance painting in the dining room, a ruby vase in the parlour. Would you like to see them?'

'Perhaps later,' hedged Orpheus. 'Sir, is a chimney sweep here by any chance? Angus Wood?'

Mayfair's eyebrows lifted a fraction. 'The sweep cleaning our parlour chimney? Yes. An urgent job, and I want him to finish as soon as possible so we can use the parlour again. Perhaps you would like to dine first, before interrupting his labours?'

Rose's stomach rumbled in reply. She blushed. Orpheus nodded fervently. The Bird Pie had been inedible.

As they followed Mayfair into the Peacock Dining Room, Orpheus's jaw dropped. The windows gleamed, brightly coloured with stained glass peacocks. Golden candlesticks shone on the tables that were covered in blue and green tablecloths. Waitresses poured tea, served cakes and whisked away plates.

A waiter soon brought them bowls of carrot soup topped with fine herbs and hot bread rolls with butter. Next came dishes of pheasant and a venison ragout. Dessert was a plate of brandy snaps with lavender custard, and cream puffs the size of dinner plates.

As they ate Rose sneaked covert looks around the dining room. She spotted the Lord Mayor, and a plump, tweed-clad man eating an enormous lunch. Mr Buttercrumbe sat nearby, reading a book titled *How to Bottle British Butterflies*. At the next table along sat a pretty young woman in lilac silk who was daintily eating a scone.

Rose beckoned to Mayfair. 'Who is that girl?'

'Miss Caroline Chippingdale,' he murmured. 'A young heiress. Her parents died when she and her brother were children. Their home was sold, and they were sent abroad. Now Miss Caroline is old enough to make a good match and has returned to Yorke. Her brother prefers the high life in Paris.' He pointed discreetly to the tweedy man. 'And that is Mr Henry Dalrymple. Owns the Braxton Food Factory. A profitable business, I am told.'

'I've heard of Braxton's. They make pickles, don't they?'

Mayfair nodded. 'Rather common pickles,' he whispered disapprovingly. 'If you have finished your meal, Master Orpheus, shall I escort you both to the parlour?'

Orpheus nodded, smiled happily down at his empty plate, and secreted a bread roll in his pocket.

It was cold in the parlour, with the fire out. There were sheets on the floor and various brushes and rods laid out.

The sweep, however, was not at his work. He was lying face-down on the floor.

Mayfair rushed over and knelt beside him. A second later he looked up at Rose and Orpheus, his expression shocked.

'Dear Lord. I – I'm afraid the poor man is dead.'

Chapter 6

The Silenced Sweep

'He was alive when I came in here only half an hour ago,' Mayfair whispered. 'How could this have happened?' He turned to the children. 'I must fetch a constable. Please, make sure no one enters the room and sees this.'

As Mayfair hurried away, Rose knelt by the body. It was not the first time she had seen a dead man but it was still deeply upsetting. She tried to keep her mind on what must be done.

'He's been hit by something,' she said, pointing to a head wound. 'Poor Mr Wood.'

'Murdered, then,' whispered Orpheus. He looked about the room. 'Who hit him? And with what, the poker? Not the coal scuttle, it's still full of coal.'

Rose inspected the poker. 'There's no sign of blood on it.'

Orpheus crouched by the body. 'There's only one door into this room.' He went to the window and pushed at the sash. 'It's shut fast. I doubt anyone slipped in or out through here.'

Rose peered out the window. 'And the snow on the ground outside is unmarked.'

She moved swiftly around the room. It contained a bookcase, a writing desk, a number of heavy, comfortable-looking chairs and two potted ferns. There was also a cabinet containing a beautiful ruby-studded vase. One of the treasures from the Yorke Museum! Very carefully Rose opened the cabinet, wrapped her fingers in a handkerchief to avoid leaving fingerprints, and looked it over closely.

'No,' she murmured. 'There's no sign that this was the weapon, either.'

'Unless the murderer cleaned it,' suggested Orpheus, coming to peer at the vase. 'Are those jewels real? How can they keep that lying about in an unlocked cabinet?'

'Well, it is the Highborne,' said Rose. 'Mayfair said they keep a Renaissance painting in the dining room. But I still don't think this was the weapon. Even if the murderer had cleaned it, I doubt they would get all the blood off.'

'Maybe someone came here to steal it!'

'Perhaps, but then why didn't they?' Rose observed. She studied the rubies again, tracing one with her finger. 'The rubies don't look right,' she muttered. One of the stones seemed to be loose in its setting. Rose took a deep breath, prised it out with her fingernail and hid it in her cameo locket.

'Rose!' Orpheus looked both shocked and impressed. 'You're going to steal it?'

'Just borrow it,' said Rose.

Orpheus shrugged. He walked to the fireplace,

peered into the hearth and squinted up the chimney.

'Anything there?' asked Rose hopefully.

'There are rungs,' he answered. 'For sweeps to use. Give me a boost and I'll climb up.'

Rose obeyed, getting soot-streaked in the process. 'People would notice someone covered in soot,' she panted, 'unless they were a chimney sweep.' She paused. 'Do you think the murderer could have climbed up the chimney to escape?'

'Not likely,' Orpheus called back. 'Too narrow. It'd be a tough job, even for a sweep. Nothing up here. Move back, and I'll jump down.'

He climbed out of the fireplace, dusting off soot. 'Rose – do you think this murder was anything to do with Inaaya going missing? Maybe Mr Wood knew something.'

'It's possible,' she replied, feeling her stomach knot. 'If only we'd spoken to him before he died!'

The door opened, making them both jump. A windblown police constable entered the room. He frowned at the sight of the children. 'What are you youngsters doing in here?' he demanded.

'It's all right, sir. Miss Raventhorpe and her friend were with me when I found the deceased,' interjected Mayfair, following after him.

The constable was not appeased. 'That's a dead body, Mr Mayfair, and this may well be a crime scene.'

'It most certainly is,' Rose told him. 'This man was hit on the head.'

Mayfair closed his eyes in distress. 'Murder, in the Highborne!'

'I'm sure we can keep it quiet,' said the police officer reassuringly. 'He's a sweep, not the Lord Mayor.'

'He was still *murdered*,' snapped Rose.

'With all due respect, Miss, I'll make that decision, not you.' He bent over the corpse. 'Hmm. He could have been choked by the soot, and hurt his head when he fell. Nasty injury. Could have been a loose brick falling out of the chimney.'

'What brick?' cried Rose. 'And if it killed him instantly, why is he lying on the carpet rather than in the fireplace?'

'People fall in funny ways,' said the constable sagely. 'As for the brick, any number of things fall down chimneys.' He scraped in the hearth with gloved fingers. 'Here we are! Bit of brick.' He held it up triumphantly.

'That's tiny,' said Rose. 'It wouldn't kill a fly. And there's no blood on it at all.'

But the officer was writing in a notebook. 'Death by work accident,' he muttered. 'Sad, but it happens. Mr Mayfair, will you see those young 'uns out? I've work to do.'

'Thank you, Constable,' said Mayfair, ushering the children out.

'He was murdered!' said Rose again, indignant.

'Yes, Miss, I'm afraid he was,' said Mayfair sadly. 'We must inform the other butlers of Silvercrest Hall. I am a Guardian of Yorke, and I have failed to stop a crime. Miss Regemont is not going to like this.'

Rose bit her lip. 'No. She isn't. But who could have entered that room once you had left it? Any of the hotel staff? The guests?'

'I would have seen any of the staff leaving the dining room,' said Mayfair. 'And any stranger entering the hotel would have been noticed. But I am sure some of the diners went out and came back. There was enough time for many of them to do the deed.'

'I hope your guests haven't left,' said Rose.

'I shall go and see,' said Mayfair. He was twisting his gloved hands together as he walked away. Rose felt sorry for him.

Mayfair returned with the tweed-suited Mr Dalrymple and the pretty Miss Caroline Chippingdale. She clutched a hatbox from Fotheringay's in one hand, and a bottle of smelling salts with the other.

'What the dash is this all about?' asked Dalrymple, dabbing gravy from his chin with a napkin. 'A chimney sweep hurt? But I'm no help at all. I'm no doctor.'

'I am afraid the man is past help,' said Mayfair. 'These children here were with me when we found him, and want to assist in the matter. We need to establish who might have seen his attacker.'

'He was murdered, then?' gasped Caroline. 'Oh, I am glad I didn't see it happen. I would faint!'

'I say,' breathed Dalrymple. He grimaced, showing horsey teeth. 'Bad luck for the hotel. Stabbed, was he?'

'Sir, please.' Mayfair's face was anguished. 'We are trying to be discreet. I'm afraid it was a blow to the head. All we need to know is if you noticed anyone leave the dining room in the past half hour. I left Mr Wood alive during that time and returned to find him dead.'

'But you can't think any of us did it!' Dalrymple looked affronted. 'It's bound to be some criminal rotter.'

'We cannot rule anyone out,' Rose explained.

'Hmm, I see,' said Dalrymple. 'Well, jolly bad luck for me. I did leave the room during that time, so I suppose I could be a suspect!' He looked amused at the idea. 'I spilled soup on my shirt, you see, so I had to go to the gentlemen's conveniences to wash it off.' He pointed to a damp spot on his shirt.

Miss Chippingdale nodded. 'I saw Mr Dalrymple coming out of the, er, powder room,' she said delicately. 'I left the dining room myself, to wash my hands and face. But I didn't meet anyone on the way.'

'Oh, I saw you, Miss,' said Dalrymple reassuringly.

'Are you sure, sir?' Caroline turned pink. 'You aren't just being gallant?'

Dalrymple beamed at her. He looked like a large boiled sweet. 'No, no, Miss. I'd remember that flowery hat anywhere.'

Orpheus glanced at the hat. It was certainly very flowery. 'Did anyone else leave the room in that time?'

Caroline considered his question. 'Yes, actually. The Countess of Dewsbury.'

'The Countess?' said Orpheus.

'I don't think we can call her a suspect,' said Rose. 'She's only seven.'

'You never know with some children,' muttered Dalrymple. 'Little hellions, they can be.'

'I rather doubt a seven year old is responsible for this crime, sir,' said Mayfair. 'However, thank you for your assistance. Now I must see to the removal of the – the unfortunate deceased.'

He walked away, the picture of dignity.

'Poor man,' murmured Caroline. 'Such a thing to happen in the Highborne! I heard him talking with the sweep when he arrived. He was rather bossy – the butler, I mean. He must feel badly about it now.'

'I imagine so,' said Orpheus.

'Thank you for talking to us,' Rose said.

'That is quite all right. I had best go,' said Caroline, picking up her silken skirts. 'I have an appointment for a ball dress fitting. You're Miss Raventhorpe, aren't you? Wait until you reach my age. You will have to dance with every eligible man in Yorke. It's very tiresome, isn't it, being expected to marry someone you might not even like?'

'Yes,' said Rose, thinking of her awful cousin. 'It definitely is.'

'Here is my calling card, if you wish to speak to me again.' She presented it to Rose, and smiled charmingly at Orpheus. He made a little bow to her.

When Caroline was gone, Rose inspected the card.

'She lives in Vicarsgate. It's a very good address. And she shops in Fotheringay's – she had a hatbox with the shop label on it. Ghastly Herbert should try to marry her instead of me!'

'I wouldn't wish that on anyone,' said Orpheus. 'Let alone a pretty girl like that. Well, those two weren't very likely suspects. We need to think about the other people in the dining room. Mr Buttercrumbe was there ... '

'And so was the Lord Mayor,' added Rose.

'He's not likely to be a murderer – he's in a bath chair!'

'You could still murder someone from a wheeled chair,' she pointed out. 'Although it would be difficult.'

Orpheus pondered it all. 'We need to talk to the butlers again,' he said. 'We still have to find Inaaya and now we also have to solve a murder.'

'Miss Rose, what happened to you?' Agnes the maid was aghast.

'Chimney,' said Rose. 'Soot. Big mess. Sorry.'

'*Chimney?*'

'Shall we go round to the kitchen entrance?' Orpheus was trying to dust soot off his coat. 'Well, I should, I'm the kitchen boy.'

'I suppose so,' said Rose. 'Sorry, Orpheus. I need to get changed, and have a bath—'

'But Miss Rose, there's a visitor for you!' said Agnes urgently.

'Now?' Rose was aghast. Then she realised it was likely to be Emily, keen to hear all the latest news. Well, Emily wouldn't mind Rose being dishevelled.

'No, Miss Rose, please—'

Rose stopped abruptly at the threshold. In the parlour, a fashionably dressed woman stood on the Turkey carpet. Her blue silk gown was trimmed with gold ruffles, while her bag was embroidered with gold flowers.

'Ah ... hello,' said Rose, discomfited. 'You wished to see me?'

'Mademoiselle Raventhorpe,' said the woman haughtily. 'I am Madame Vidoux. I come to make your wedding dress.'

Chapter 7

RUBY AND GARNET

'My *wedding dress?*'

This was a nightmare.

It had to be a nightmare.

'You are not a beauty like your Mama,' said Madame Vidoux, eyeing Rose critically, 'But you will do. A few more years, yes, they give the magic. *Les Anglaises*, they have not ze style of French women but My Lady Raventhorpe, she is *magnifique*. She wears furs like a Russian.'

'This is ridiculous!' spluttered Rose.

'*Attends, Mademoiselle*, I do not pay ze visit to many. A duchess, a princess – maybe. But I know your mama. For *La Belle Lady Raventhorpe*, I make ze exception.'

'Does my mother know you are here?' Rose demanded.

'I promised your parents to make you some dresses,' said Madame Vidoux, unpacking a sketch book from her bag. 'But I will start on ze wedding dress now, before I am too booked up.'

Rose cleared her throat. 'I'm sorry, but I'm only twelve. I'm not marrying anyone.'

Madame Vidoux shrugged. 'Many book me years in advance. I am in demand. I make ze gown for a countess when she is no more than ten. Zat girl grows to look like a horse, but when he see her in my gown, ze groom cry with joy.'

'But I . . . you see— '

'Measurements!' cried Madame. She rose to her feet just as Agnes brought in a tray of cakes. '*Non*. Mademoiselle eats no cakes until she is married.'

'What?'

'You want ze dress to fit, no? I make allowances for when you grow,' said Madame. She was measuring Rose's figure expertly with a smart red tape measure that had appeared from her bag. She turned Rose around and started sketching in a small book. 'Long sleeves here, and embroidered stars. And a train, a Raventhorpe must have a train.'

'But I'm not getting married!'

Agnes quickly departed just as Herbert walked in.

'Oh splendid,' he said pompously. 'The dress is arranged. Yes, very suitable.' He turned to Rose and lifted an eyebrow. 'Hmm, maybe Madame should do something with your current outfit as well. You're a mess!'

Rose's eyes flashed.

'I am not marrying you. Not now. Not *ever*.'

Herbert strolled round to the sofa. 'Actually, we should look into the flower arrangements.'

'*Actually*, I'm not getting married,' said Rose.

'The train should be longer,' said Herbert,

studying Madame's sketch. 'Rose will have ten bridesmaids, including my sister Marjorie. She doesn't like Rose at all, but she has agreed to do the invitation list and organise the music.'

As Heddsworth came in with a pot of tea, he looked over Madame's shoulder at the sketch. 'How charming,' he said. 'What will you wear with it, Master Herbert?'

Herbert gave him a withering look. 'You belong in the kitchen, not out here with your betters.'

'Certainly, young sir. And perhaps Miss Rose should go upstairs and have a wash?'

'Thank you, Heddsworth. I shall,' said Rose, accepting a cup of tea from him. 'Thank you for your attentions, Madame – good day to you.'

'A wedding dress, Heddsworth! She's making me a wedding dress!'

Rose was storming about her bedroom.

Heddsworth was dusting the piano in the corner. 'Most exasperating, Miss Raventhorpe,' he agreed.

'Though I must say Madame is a superb dress designer. She makes some of Miss Regemont's gowns.'

'That's not the point! You don't want me to marry Herbert, do you?'

'Assuredly not, Miss Raventhorpe.'

She paused. 'Have you duelled Bixby yet?'

'No. But he is still looking forward to having me sacked.'

Rose crossed her arms. 'I would rather lock myself up in this room till doomsday than see either of them again.'

'Now really, Miss Raventhorpe. From what you have told me, we now have a murder to solve. And a missing child to find.'

'Yes,' said Rose, striving to compose herself. 'Sorry. Quite right. I need to go to Locks and Clocks to ask them about this so-called ruby.' She opened her locket, and showed it to Heddsworth.

'It does look suspiciously fake,' he agreed. 'While you do that, I shall send word to the Hall about poor

Angus Wood. The Ravens are going to be upset, no doubt about that.'

'Good afternoon, Mr Goldsmith.'

Rose had entered the shop hoping to see Garnet but there was still no sign of her. Mr Goldsmith and Sapphire were packing a carriage clock into a box. 'I wondered if you would look at this ruby for me,' Rose asked. 'Oh – are you all right?'

Mr Goldsmith looked terrible. His curly hair was uncombed, his skin pale grey. When he tried to smile at Rose, she started. Mr Goldsmith's gold teeth were missing.

'What happened to your teeth?'

He waved a hand. 'Nothing to worry about, Miss. We're going through a very busy period.'

'So I see.' Rose now noticed that half the displays in the shop had vanished. Many of the velvet caskets used for displaying jewellery were empty.

'Is Garnet still unwell?' Rose enquired. 'Are there medical costs?'

'No!' cried Mr Goldsmith. 'Not at all. She's just not up to seeing visitors. What did you want help with, Miss?'

Uneasily, Rose showed him the ruby. 'I don't think this is genuine.'

Goldsmith picked it up and narrowed his eyes. 'No,' he said. 'No, it's only glass. I do hope that is not a disappointment, Miss Raventhorpe.'

'Not at all,' Rose assured him. 'Do you need help of any kind?'

There was a long pause. Mr Goldsmith looked away.

'No,' he said. 'Thank you, but no.'

Rose went straight to Silvercrest Hall where she was shown to Miss Regemont's office. Bronson and Charlie Malone were summoned.

'Murder at the Highborne.' Miss Regemont swished about the room in a whirl of crimson silk. 'Mayfair is distraught. And the sweeps will be furious.'

'Then we need to find out who did it,' said Bronson, pacing in front of the fireplace. 'And fast. It sounds like you and Orpheus did a fine job of investigating the scene, Miss Raventhorpe. Who is your prime suspect? Do you think it was a case of thievery?'

Rose held out the false ruby. 'I think this has something to do with it. The vase on display at the Highborne is not genuine.'

Charlie Malone frowned. 'You mean the museum lent the hotel a fake?'

'No, I'm sure Mayfair would have noticed,' said Miss Regemont. 'It sounds as if a thief may have stolen the real vase and left a copy. A clever ruse. But was it done at the time of the murder? And who is the thief?'

'That is not the only mystery. Something is going on at Locks and Clocks,' Rose insisted. 'We need to find out what's happened to Garnet.'

Bronson glanced at her, eyebrows raised. 'You don't think Miss Goldsmith is really ill?'

'No, I'm sure the Goldsmiths are lying.'

Miss Regemont frowned. 'Perhaps she has run away from home. There may have been a family argument. I know Miss Garnet and her father do not always agree.'

'Still, why keep it secret?' Charlie Malone demanded. 'The truth would be embarrassing for the family, I'm sure, but they would be worried to death about her. Plus they know we would help, and be discreet about it.'

Bronson nodded. 'Yes, but we need to ensure that Garnet is genuinely missing before we ransack the whole of Yorke. And there is still Inaaya Rayburn to find.'

'I wish the Raven Society was still friendly with us,' said Miss Regemont with a sigh. 'A sweep might know something. They can go where we cannot. Very agile, sweeps.'

Rose paused. 'I could send Watchful to look around. He's a Guardian, like the rest of us. In the meantime, can you keep searching for Inaaya? Not just in the Muckyards – she may be somewhere else in the city. Or in a mill, like the one Orpheus was sent to.'

Miss Regemont nodded. 'We shall indeed. Mr Malone, what are you doing with that fake ruby?'

Charlie Malone was holding it up to the light. 'Just thinking it was pretty,' he said brightly. 'Pity it isn't real. You could use it in an engagement ring, Miss Raventhorpe.'

'Very funny,' said Rose, annoyed. 'I'm not getting married.' *But Heddsworth could be sacked*, said a nasty voice in her mind. *And if he is, it will be your fault.*

Chapter 8

An Unkindness of Ravens

Snow was falling as the carriage pulled up outside Locks and Clocks.

'I know it's cold outside, Watchful, but I need your help. Can you climb up to the window ledge above the shop and see if Garnet is in her bedroom? I suppose you know what a bedroom is. You are a Guardian . . .'

Watchful blinked and yawned. Rose hoped she was not making a fool of herself by talking to this cat. She climbed down to the street with Watchful in her arms.

'Off you go then,' she said encouragingly.

She wondered if he understood her at all. He sniffed disdainfully at the cold air, and gave Rose a reproachful look. He made no attempt to escape her arms.

'I'm sorry,' she whispered. 'But you're a Guardian, and we need to do this.' She set him down on a patch of dirty snow.

'Go on, Watchful,' she pleaded. 'The butlers need your help. If you don't want to, can any of the other cats of Yorke do it? I'll give you a haddock for dinner.'

She wasn't sure if the haddock was the reason, but Watchful suddenly seemed to notice the shopfront. He leapt upwards.

As Rose glanced around her for any dogs, Watchful bounded from window ledge to window ledge. Pausing for a moment he balanced on top of the dragon statue above the doorway to Locks and Clocks. Then he stepped daintily up on to the ledge above. The window was open, and he dived through it.

106

Rose waited nervously. She could have returned to the carriage to stay warm and out of sight, but it seemed more loyal to stand in the cold and wait.

At last Watchful reappeared. He zigzagged down the ledges and rubbed his back on Rose's skirt.

'Well?' Rose whispered. 'Was she there?'

The cat hissed softly. His tail flicked. Then Rose saw he had something in his teeth. He lowered his head and dropped it into her gloved hand.

It was Garnet's silver charm bracelet, hung with tokens of the jeweller's trade – a miniature anvil, pliers, and a vice.

Dread crept outwards from Rose's heart to her fingertips. Something bad had happened to Garnet, she was sure of it. Somehow she had to find her, and help the Goldsmiths.

Later, back in her room, Rose hid her rapier under the bed and went to the fire to warm herself.

A lump tumbled out of the coals towards her.

Rose grabbed the tongs, picked it up, and dropped it into the coal scuttle.

It was a broken cup handle.

The Ravens wanted to talk.

Rose woke at midnight when Watchful jumped on to her bed. She was mumbling a protest when she heard a tap at her door.

'I am very sorry to wake you, Miss Raventhorpe,' whispered Heddsworth. 'But I have received word we are to meet the Ravens on the city wall.'

Rose sat up blearily in bed. 'Now?' she said. 'Why this late at night? Why a wall?'

'They would rather not hold this meeting in public,' said Heddsworth. 'And they will not set foot in the Hall. A pity, as it is remarkably cold. Here is your warmest coat and your boots. Master Orpheus is dressing downstairs.'

Rose wore her rapier. This sounded like a mission that might require it.

She and Heddsworth crept downstairs where

they met Orpheus in the kitchen. Despite his obvious worry about Inaaya, he looked excited by the midnight adventure. They slipped through the window of the butlers' pantry and set off, by lantern light, towards the walls of the city.

Tired and cold as she was, Rose was glad to climb up the stone steps to the city wall. The wall was one of her favourite things about Yorke.

They reached the battlements, and began to walk. 'They'll find us soon enough,' Heddsworth remarked.

Rose and Orpheus gazed out over the city, lit now only by gas lamps and candles. Snow fell softly along the walls. Rose's teeth chattered.

'It's beautiful up here,' murmured Orpheus. 'I never saw the city like this before.'

Suddenly Rose saw torchlight moving towards them on the wall. Heddsworth's hand shifted automatically to his rapier. 'Fawney?' he called.

In answer, the sweep lifted his burning torch so they could see his face. A group of fellow sweeps stood behind him. All were armed with fireplace pokers.

'Wood was murdered, wasn't he?' asked Fawney.

'We believe so,' said Rose.

'By that butler! That Mayfair!' cried a sweep.

'Where is he?' shouted another. 'We'll make him pay for Angus!'

'We have no proof that Mayfair has harmed anyone. Nor do we suspect him,' argued Heddsworth.

'That's right,' said a sweep bitterly. 'Protect your own.'

'We are investigating the crime,' Heddsworth insisted. 'And we need your help to do so.'

'We do want justice for Angus Wood!' cried Rose. 'He might have witnessed a robbery, which led to his death.'

One sweep stormed forward with his poker held high. Rose drew her rapier and stood waiting, wary.

The sweep lowered his weapon. 'Ah, I can't fight a wee girl.'

Heddsworth stepped forward and took the poker from him before dropping it loudly on the stone. Orpheus unclenched his fists.

'None of us want to fight,' said Heddsworth. 'We came to talk.'

The raven on Fawney's shoulder flapped its wings. 'Get on wi' it then,' grunted Fawney. 'Talk.'

Rose drew a breath. 'Tell us more about Angus Wood. Did he have any enemies? Why would anyone want to hurt him?'

'Angus didn't 'ave no enemies,' grunted Fawney. 'Did good work. Been in the trade since he were a sprat.'

'Then why would Mayfair do him any harm?' demanded Rose.

'Could be anythin',' said Fawney obstinately. 'You butlers don't like us. And you got your weapons.'

'Angus Wood was struck on the head, not stabbed with a rapier,' said Heddsworth. 'Nor was he shot.'

'Makes no difference,' snapped another sweep. 'Dead is dead.'

111

Rose bit her lip. 'But he might have seen or heard something important.'

Fawney glared at Rose and her friends. 'Then you needs to find out what that somethin' is. 'Cause if you don't, the chimneys o' this city will be choked up, and it's a cold winter, Miss Raventhorpe.'

He nodded to the walls of the city. Rose saw torchlights all around the walls. The sweeps of Yorke were standing vigil.

'How long are you giving us?' Heddsworth inquired.

'A week,' said Fawney.

'A week?' sputtered Orpheus.

'We can make it less,' another sweep snarled.

'Fine. A week is fine,' said Heddsworth. 'We shall endeavour to find out the truth. And if Mayfair is indeed responsible, we shall inform the authorities. We will not shield a murderer.'

The sweeps scowled, but Fawney nodded tersely.

'There's something else I need to ask,' Rose put in. 'We have a number of suspects regarding Wood's murder. Do you know if Angus Wood had any connections to the Lord Mayor? The taxidermist Mr Buttercrumbe? Mr Henry Dalrymple?'

Fawney snorted. 'Wood's worked for nearly everyone in Yorke. I read the ashes for you, Missy, and Wood ended up dead. It's up to you to fix things.'

'But—'

'Wait,' said Fawney. 'Dalrymple, you said? Owns the factory? You could talk to him. He might know summat. But a hard job that'll be. He's a secretive feller.'

He led the sweeps away. The torchlight across the city began to move and disappear in trails of smoke.

Heddsworth folded his arms. 'Right. We had better get on with it. It sounds like Mr Dalrymple is worth talking to.'

'I will do it,' said Rose resolutely. 'He might be secretive about his factory, but he will let me in, whether he likes it or not.'

Chapter 9

Facts at the Factory

With Orpheus busy in the kitchen, Rose decided to ask her friend Emily to visit the Braxton Food Factory with her. Emily, it turned out, was delighted.

'Dalrymple is reputed to be good at his business,' she told Rose, as they rode in Emily's carriage along Ravensgate. 'Mama considered I marry him once. I'm so glad I didn't, though, I doubt he would appreciate the dark and tragic beauty of Gothic literature. What will we say when we talk to him?'

'We'll tell him we are seeking patrons for my father's charities. Hopefully that will get us in the door.'

'I know!' Emily sat up, her purple hat nearly slipping off her curls. 'Our hot air balloon – the one we took on our honeymoon! We can tell Dalrymple we're thinking of placing advertisements on it. Say that we would like to promote the factory.'

'Brilliant!' cheered Rose. 'But would you really do that?'

'Advertise pickles on our lovely balloon?' Emily made a face. 'No. I'd rather have lovely Gothic poetry written on it. Or, it would be a nice way to advertise the Clarion Theatre and Harry's acts, wouldn't it?'

The carriage turned down another street, passing schools, offices, and warehouses. It drew to a stop at a big, mustard-coloured building. Yellowy-green smoke poured up from its chimneys. Rose and Emily wrinkled their noses at the smell.

The girls knocked on the factory door but the

115

noise of the machinery inside was so loud they doubted anyone would hear them. Emily resorted to thumping the door with her parasol. Finally a workman came to the door and stared at them in surprise. Rose explained her visit. 'I do apologise for appearing unannounced,' she said sweetly. 'But I am sure Mr Dalrymple would welcome us, as a benefactor of the city.'

The workman let them in, and asked them to wait. The girls winced at the heat and smell of the room. It was all steel pipes and boxes and bottles, and workers in drab clothes turning wheels, packing up boxes and polishing machinery. Gloop poured out of one spout into jars, the same yellowish-green as the smoke. The workers were too busy to give them many curious looks.

When the workman reappeared he beckoned to the girls. 'Mr Dalrymple says you can come up, Misses. This way. Watch your step.'

They climbed a flight of stairs and entered a tidy office with a carpet, a fire and a small table set for tea. Mr Dalrymple himself, clad in his customary tweed, came forward to greet them.

'Young ladies! What a surprise! I hardly ever have guests. I am astonished that a pair of sweet little creatures like yourselves would come to my grimy old factory.'

Rose put on her most innocent expression.

'My father, Lord Raventhorpe, is very interested in Yorke industry,' she said, trying to sound shy and earnest. 'He is seeking support for his charities, especially during this terrible winter. He has asked me to invite generous local businessmen to become patrons. The charities organise food, clothing and coal for the poor.'

'Ah, now that is a suitable thing for a young lady,' said Dalrymple approvingly. 'Kindness to the poor. I should be delighted to help. We can provide food for your charity! Now, you are just in time for tea. How do you like what you have seen of the factory? I don't suppose you are interested in machinery. Terribly dull for girls.'

'It's very interesting,' said Rose. She and Emily sat down on a creaking sofa, while Dalrymple poured tea. 'Everyone seems to be working very hard.'

'That's the idea,' said Dalrymple heartily. 'Have to keep everything strictly on schedule and clean as a whistle. No shirking on my watch! Here, have something to eat.'

Rose and Emily flinched at the sight of the offerings. There were green crab-paste sandwiches, cups of murky tea and flat, tough cream buns.

'I'm planning to expand the place, once I've perfected my new recipes,' Dalrymple informed the girls. 'In fact I'm hoping to get a Royal Warrant. We shall provide fine jams, preserved fruits, foie gras and other delicacies. Better than Dorabella's Tea Shop by a mile! We shall be the Fortnum's of the North.'

Emily choked on her tea. 'Ugh!' she whispered to Rose as Dalrymple bit into a cream bun. 'It's like Thames river water!'

'That sounds marvellous,' Rose told Dalrymple. 'You must be a splendid businessman to have thought of all that! My goodness, how long and hard you must have worked. Years and years!'

'Oh, one works hard,' said Dalrymple modestly, showing his horsey teeth. 'I bought this place over ten years ago, when it was still a very small factory. Made pickles. Decent profits, but much of it goes into paying the workers, and there are other costs that might be difficult for young ladies to comprehend. In the meantime, I have worked on special recipes for new foodstuffs.'

'Special recipes?' said Rose. 'Like these, er, teatime treats?'

Dalrymple nodded. 'Of course, I am always tweaking recipes. I test everything thoroughly.'

'Exactly what Father would like,' said Rose. 'It all sounds very proper. Do you let anyone taste the foods?'

Dalrymple smiled, and sipped tea. 'I must keep my secrets, Miss Raventhorpe! But I do have reliable testers, especially for the baby food.'

Rose wrinkled her nose. 'Baby food?'

'Yes,' said Dalrymple eagerly. 'A splendid new product. For infants around the nation. A young lady with a fine inheritance would do well to invest in local industry one day.'

'And we can offer some excellent advertising,' said Emily, describing her balloon idea.

'A balloon?' Dalrymple drummed his fingers on his chin. 'Intriguing ... How modern! Go on.'

'Excuse me, Mr Dalrymple?' said Rose. 'Do you have a room where I might wash my face? I'm feeling rather dusty.'

'Eh? Oh yes. Use my own. Down there. First room on the left.' He smiled toothily. 'Don't get lost, now! Dangerous places, factories.'

'Oh, I quite agree.' Rose smoothed down her dress fussily and set off towards the lavatory.

She did actually need to use it, so that was a convenient excuse. Business taken care of, she sought the best way to have a good snoop round the factory. She could still hear Emily chatting about ballooning in the office behind her.

Rose tiptoed to the window. From here she could hear the noise of the factory machinery, and was glad it muffled her footsteps. She peered out, pushing aside the cheap curtains.

The window overlooked a courtyard. Grey-clad workers were crossing it, loading up a wagon with heavy boxes of Braxton Foods products. Some of the workers looked terribly young.

Rose tried to open the window, but it was locked. She watched for as long as she dared. Then, chagrined, she returned to Emily and Dalrymple.

'It was so kind of you to allow us to visit,' she told Dalrymple in her most cordial tones. 'What do you think of the balloon idea? Isn't it grand? Well, we've taken enough of your time. Shall we show ourselves out, Emily? We mustn't bother Mr Dalrymple when he is so busy.'

'No trouble at all. I shall escort you, young ladies. Pleasure all mine.' Dalrymple heaved himself up off the chair. 'Here, you can take some free food samples with you.'

'Oh, lovely!' faltered Emily, taking the box.

The roar of the factory returned as they went downstairs, as did the smell of metal and oil and sour cabbage. Jars clinked on a production line. The workers in this enormous room were all adult. Rose thought fast.

'Mr Dalrymple, this is such a fascinating place! Might Emily and I talk to some of the workers? I've never talked to a factory worker before. Father would like it, I'm sure.'

One of the good things about being a lord's daughter was the influence people felt when Lord Frederick was mentioned. Dalrymple immediately stood up straighter.

'Very well then, Miss Raventhorpe. Here! You!' He beckoned to one of the workers, a gaunt man who looked terrified. He crept towards his master.

'Aye, sir?'

'Tell this young lady how good it is to work here.' There was a warning edge to Dalrymple's voice and his cheery demeanour was gone.

'Ar,' said the man uneasily. 'Grand. Just grand.'

'How lovely,' said Rose, with a pained glance at Emily.

Emily took the cue. 'My goodness, is the wheel supposed to turn like that?' she asked, pointing further down the room. 'It looks wobbly to me.'

Dalrymple strode off in the direction she was indicating. 'Wobbly? Where?'

Rose leaned forward. 'Sir,' she said to the worker, under the clatter of machinery. 'Are there children working here? Where are they from?'

The man glanced nervously at Dalrymple who was snapping orders at his staff.

'Them? They're just stray bairns, Miss. Dalrymple gets 'em in. We don't talk to 'em much. Ain't allowed.'

'Where do they live? What do they do?'

'Pack boxes, Miss. They live down in the cellar.'

'Is one of them called Inaaya? A girl of about six? Her mother was from India, and her father—'

'They're mostly boys, Miss. Ain't seen no

foreigners.' The man stepped away fearfully. 'I can't say no more, Miss.'

Dalrymple came steaming back. 'Nothing wrong with it, as I thought. Right, you hop back to it,' he told the worker. 'I trust you are ready to leave, young ladies?'

'Yes, thank you,' said Emily. 'We appreciate your gift of food samples.'

'Do tell me if your families are interested in investing in the company,' Dalrymple called, as they went back to their carriage. 'It's a most profitable concern.'

'We shall certainly think about it,' said Emily. 'Won't we, Rose?'

'Oh yes,' said Rose. 'You have definitely given us something to think about.'

Back in the carriage, Rose plumped down in her seat and scowled. 'Beastly man – using small children for heavy work like that!'

'It's awfully common, I'm afraid,' said Emily. 'I hope he isn't treating them too harshly.'

'It's detestable,' said Rose. 'But I didn't see any girl that looked like Inaaya. Perhaps she isn't here. But I'd like to tell Father about those children and see if Dalrymple is breaking the law.'

She looked across at the box of samples in Emily's lap. 'Of course, he could be a murderer as well. But if he did kill Wood, we haven't established a motive.' She took a jar of baby food from the box, and opened the lid. 'This looks disgusting! Just smell it, ugh. It's nothing more than green gloop. I wouldn't let an adult near it, let alone a baby!' She paused. Something nudged at her memory.

'Now that I think of it, Orpheus had to eat horrible green food at the orphanage. You don't suppose it was this stuff? Dalrymple did say he tested it on people. How awful – he probably tests it on orphans!'

'Urgh,' said Emily. 'Those poor orphans! I suppose it's cheap for the orphanage to buy.'

'It's a connection to Bleakstone,' said Rose thoughtfully. She turned the jar round in her hands.

'If his food made them sick, or killed them, who would know?'

'But Rose, Orpheus didn't say Inaaya got sick, did he? He would surely have noticed if she did. And wouldn't the orphans have told you if she was unwell?'

'That's true. Corrie didn't say Inaaya was ill,' said Rose, remembering. 'Some of them did look poorly, though. I still think there is some sort of connection. Here, give me those food samples. I want to show them to Orpheus.'

When she arrived home, Rose's clothes still smelled faintly of the factory. Agnes insisted on drawing her a bath. As she gathered an armful of soaps and bath salts, she said:

'I'm sorry, Miss, but can I have a word?'

'Yes, of course,' said Rose, opening a window to air out her room.

Agnes looked tense. 'Things 'as been goin' missing in the house, Miss.'

'Missing?' Rose stared at her. 'What things?'

'Some of the silver,' whispered Agnes. 'And a crystal vase from M'Lady's bedroom. I swear it wasn't me, Miss!'

'Of course it wasn't,' said Rose, shocked. 'Has Mother said anything?'

'She's asked where those things are. I said I'd look for them, and I have, but . . .'

Rose had a nasty suspicion. 'Have you looked in Herbert's room?'

'Aye,' whispered Agnes. 'But I can't stay long in there, Miss. And he's got a locked trunk, I couldn't check that.'

'Right,' said Rose. 'Leave it to me.'

Orpheus met her downstairs. 'Quick,' he whispered. 'Listen. They're in the parlour.'

Rose didn't ask who 'they' were. She followed on tiptoe, and listened at the door. Herbert was talking to Lady Constance.

'If you ask me, your butler's very suspicious,'

Herbert declared. 'Too quick-fingered. Several of my things have gone missing. My silver-plated shoehorn, a pair of gloves, a snuffbox, and a miniature of my sister Marjorie. I want the servants' quarters searched!'

'Have you asked your butler about them?' asked Her Ladyship. 'I am sure none of our servants would resort to thievery. The very idea!'

'You can't trust anyone in service,' warned Herbert. 'That maid Agnes doesn't know her place either – she is always talking in a familiar way with Rose.'

'Well Agnes is a country girl,' said Lady Constance. 'Not a Londoner. I shall speak to Heddsworth about the missing items, however.'

'The search should be carried out now!'

'He must have planted them in Heddsworth's room!' hissed Rose.

'Or gotten Bixby to do it,' muttered Orpheus.

'I'm afraid the matter will have to wait,' they heard Lady Constance say. 'I have to pay a call to friends in Vicarsgate. When I return I shall discuss it with his Lordship.'

Rose and Orpheus hid themselves from view as Lady Constance swept out. As soon as she was gone, they dashed into the parlour.

'Herbert, you sneak! You're framing Heddsworth for theft!' hissed Rose.

Herbert stared. Then he crossed his arms.

'It's not my fault he's a thief. And it isn't seemly in my future wife to eavesdrop. Nor should we have discussions like this in front of the domestics.' He gave Orpheus a nasty look. Orpheus brushed down his kitchen attire. 'Just helping Miss Rose, *sir.*'

Watchful the cat paced into the room and curled himself around Rose's skirts. Then he turned about, ran into the hall and leaped lightly upstairs. Rose and Orpheus followed the cat, with Herbert protesting in their wake.

The cat entered Herbert's room ('get out of here!') and pawed at the locked trunk.

'Where does he keep the key?' Rose asked the cat.

Watchful leaped on to the bedside table, where Herbert kept a biscuit tin. He nudged it with his nose.

Herbert dived for the tin but Rose was quicker. She grabbed the tin, tugged off the lid and took out a key.

'You should drown that cat,' Herbert snarled. But he dared not step closer, not with Orpheus and Watchful in his way. Rose unlocked the trunk and took out a letter.

'Dear Papa,' she read out loud, 'Servants here completely useless, but I am taking care of that. I'll have them discharged by the end of the week, with Bixby's help. I also asked Bixby to have a look around Lord F's study. You were right. He's trying to change another law, which will stop you from building that railway through the village. Completely unfair and unreasonable.'

'Stop reading my private letter!' Herbert tried to get past Orpheus. 'It's not suitable behaviour for my future wife!'

'I am not your future wife!' Rose almost shouted. 'You framed our servants, didn't you? You got Bixby to hide some of your things in their room, so you could run to my parents and accuse our staff of being thieves! The imaginary engagement is off.'

That brought a nasty smile from Herbert. 'Then I'll tell your parents about your friends at that Silvercrest Hall place. And the swords. And about *him*.' He pointed at Orpheus. 'He's a runaway orphan, isn't he? The dirty urchin who interrupted the cathedral service! He should go back to the gutter.'

'Just try it,' snapped Rose. 'And I'll tell my father what you've done. Sneaking and spying, trying to stop Father changing laws! You do what we say, Herbert, or I show my father that letter.'

'Do what?' Herbert snarled. 'Apologise to dear Mr Heddsworth?'

'For a start,' replied Rose. 'And you can give up your mad marriage idea. You can keep quiet about the butlers too. We need to investigate a murder and find Orpheus's sister.'

Herbert's nose twitched in outrage. 'Investigate a ... let you ... not in a thousand years!'

'Are you going to agree or shall I send Orpheus to fetch Father?'

A minute ticked by in silence.

'Fine,' Herbert muttered at last. 'I'll let you do your stupid *investigation*.'

'Good. You can come with us,' said Rose. 'So I can keep an eye on you. You're not going to do any more harm to Heddsworth or you'll find out what happens when you really upset a Raventhorpe.'

Chapter 10

The Mystery of Mayfair

'I don't understand,' whined Herbert, as he rode with Heddsworth, Rose and Orpheus in the carriage to the Highborne. 'Why do we have to see your stupid butler friends at the hotel? What's wrong with their fancy Hall?'

'We all need to talk to Mayfair, the hotel butler,' said Rose. 'Heddsworth received a message saying he was in a state.'

Heddsworth consulted his fob watch. 'Miss Regemont said twelve o'clock. I do like being punctual.'

They entered the golden doors of the hotel. Mayfair stood in his customary place but there was a tense wariness in his expression. He smiled in relief when he saw the new arrivals.

'Miss Regemont and the other butlers are waiting for you in the alcove,' he said, with a wave of his hand. 'I shall be glad to join you.'

The 'alcove' was a private nook of the dining room. There they found Miss Regemont sat in a red velvet chair while Charlie Malone and Bronson shared a window seat, eating scones with blackberry jam. Bronson swallowed her mouthful of scone and moved over to make room for the children. 'Now, Mayfair,' she said, 'What can we do to help you? The sweeps think you are to blame for poor Mr Wood's fate but we know you better than that.'

'I had nothing to do with it, Madam!' Mayfair protested. 'I am perfectly innocent!'

'Is there more cake?' asked Herbert, his mouth full of scone.

'Miss Chippingdale said you were talking to Mr

134

Wood before his death, Mayfair,' said Rose. 'Being bossy, as she put it.'

'With Mr Wood?' Mayfair frowned. 'He was rather surly, it's true – I asked him to do the job as quickly as possible. But I would hardly call that bossy. And it was no cause for murder!' He wrung his hands. 'I know some people believe I did it. This morning,' he whispered, 'I received this in the post.'

He took something from inside his jacket pocket. It was a pretty embossed gingerbread tin from Dorabella's Tea Shop. Mayfair opened it.

There was a marzipan base with gingerbread letter shapes stuck into it. Rose had seen such gifts before. They usually spelled out 'Happy Birthday!' or 'Be My Valentine'.

These letters lined up to spell M-U-R-D-E-R-E-R. Everyone sat frozen.

'Mmm, gingerbread,' said Herbert, reaching for a biscuit. Rose thwacked his fingers with the tin lid.

Heddsworth's hand was on the hilt of his rapier. 'What kind of coward does this?'

'One of the sweeps, I expect,' said Bronson.

'Could be anyone,' said Charlie sadly. 'I mean, rumours fly. Half of Yorke probably believes it now.'

'I should resign,' whispered Mayfair.

'No you shouldn't!' Bronson retorted. 'It would make you look guilty! And you're not.'

'But I can't prove it!'

Miss Regemont stood up and placed her hand on his. 'We are all behind you, Mayfair. Understand that.'

'Thank you, Madam. I'm most grateful.' Mayfair cleared his throat. 'I had better get on with collecting flowers from the conservatory. I shall be there if I am required.'

After he departed, the group sat in despairing silence. Herbert ate blackberry jam from the jar with a spoon.

'Poor man,' said Miss Regemont. 'What can we do?'

'Work out what we know,' said Rose. 'We know

that the murderer was probably a thief. That they were in the hotel that day. It may have been Mr Dalrymple, who is looking to expand his business. He might need the money.'

'Is he desperate enough to become a thief?' Miss Regemont sounded doubtful.

'He employs children in his factory,' said Orpheus. 'And supplies Bleakstone with disgusting food. We ate that baby food of his.'

'That doesn't make him a murderer,' Bronson pointed out. 'He sounds like a rather typical factory owner.'

'Have you found any sign of Inaaya?' Orpheus asked.

'No,' said Bronson. 'I'm sorry. We have looked, Orpheus.'

Orpheus looked at the floor. 'Thank you for trying.'

'We haven't seen any signs of Garnet Goldsmith either,' added Bronson.

Rose took Garnet's bracelet from her pocket.

'Watchful found this. She would never have left it behind on purpose. I'm sure she's missing too.'

'Fine lot of Guardians we are,' said Charlie Malone, staring moodily at his teacup. 'Missing children, a murdered sweep. We need to act! Spread the word round the butlers in Yorke. Ask them if they know anything, have heard anything, seen anything.'

Miss Regemont nodded. 'Criminals make mistakes. Something will come to light soon, surely.'

'Real butlers,' drawled Herbert, 'know their places. Bixby certainly does.'

Rose stood up, tossing her napkin to the table. 'I'll duel Bixby myself if you won't be quiet. Orpheus, let's ask Mayfair if he noticed Mr Dalrymple acting suspiciously. Herbert, try to do something useful for a change!'

Herbert rolled his eyes, and took another scone.

Rose and Orpheus headed for the conservatory. The hotel grew all its flowers in a beautiful glass hothouse. It was richly scented, and deliciously warm.

Rose listened for the sounds of snipping scissors or flower-arranging. But the conservatory was silent.

'Bother,' said Rose. 'Mayfair isn't here.'

Orpheus made a choking noise. Rose looked where he pointed.

Mayfair lay face down on the floor, surrounded by a handful of flowers. His head was bloody. Beside him lay a fireplace poker.

Chapter 11

Flinty's Fakery

The butlers of Silvercrest Hall were outraged by Mayfair's murder. As far as most of them were concerned the Raven Society was responsible. The chimney sweeps were equally sure that Mayfair had killed Angus Wood. Both factions travelled about Yorke in groups, armed with their favourite weapons. Ashes and sand were poured down chimneys. No butler went near the Muckyards if they could help it.

Miss Regemont was at her wits' end. 'We cannot

duel them. It is not behaviour worthy of the Guardians of Yorke!' she kept insisting. 'There will be no bloodshed. No scuffles in the street. I will not have it.'

But it had been a week since the sweeps had given their warning. Now the chimneys of the city would slowly choke up, while the weather grew colder and colder each day.

Rose was increasingly anxious to find out who had murdered Angus Wood. She needed to talk to every suspect. After some thought, she decided to visit Mr Buttercrumbe again. He might have seen something important at the Highborne.

Mr Buttercrumbe was whistling as he rearranged his window displays. Across the street, Rose and Orpheus watched him dusting an aardvark he had acquired from a London zoo. Next to this he had lined up parrots, magpies and canaries to resemble a choir, the birds holding sheet music while a nightingale in front held a tiny baton in its feathers.

Rose and Orpheus came in. 'Good morning!' cried Buttercrumbe. 'I thought some colour would liven up this dreary weather. What do you think of the display?'

'Er – very nice,' said Rose. 'Mr Buttercrumbe, we noticed you dining at the Highborne a week ago. Do you remember?'

'I certainly do,' beamed Buttercrumbe. 'It was my birthday, and I was treating myself to roast goose. I think the hotel might consider buying some of my work. A genuine peacock in the dining room would give it extra style, don't you think?'

'Maybe,' said Orpheus unconvincingly. 'I don't know, sir. I'm not sure I'd want one staring at me while I was eating.'

'Fine birds, peacocks,' Buttercrumbe went on. 'Can I help you at all?'

'Oh, yes,' said Rose. 'Did you know that a sweep was murdered that day at the Highborne?'

'Ah! I heard about that.' Buttercrumbe paused. 'Terrible news.'

For an unpleasant moment Rose thought Buttercrumbe might express a desire to preserve Angus Wood's body. Thankfully he did not, so she went on. 'Mr Mayfair is dead now too. We thought you might have seen or heard something that would help find the murderer.'

He nodded soberly. 'I see. Well, I don't understand who would want to hurt either of the poor chaps.' Then he gasped.

'What?' cried Rose and Orpheus.

'That gives me an idea for a new display! A judge and jury with a bloodhound tricked out in a white wig, a magpie as prosecutor and a handsome black cat as a butler! I think it would be a sensation.'

'Ah, yes. Eye opening,' said Orpheus, seeing Rose's stunned expression. 'Remarkable. The thing is, sir, we hoped you might have seen or heard something suspicious the day you were at the hotel.

Did you see anyone leave the dining room or go to the parlour?'

Buttercrumbe reflected, polishing a beady bird eye with his sleeve.

'Hmm, hard to remember. The Lord Mayor didn't budge, I'm sure. That bath chair of his would be easy to notice. The pretty young lady went out, perhaps. A few of the men.'

'Caroline Chippingdale did,' agreed Rose. 'Mr Dalrymple confirmed it.'

'I remember the young lady's hatbox. I wished I could have seen the hat – small birds are very popular on hats. I have a standing order at Fotheringay's, you know.'

'How lovely,' said Rose, deciding to avoid all hats with birds on them. 'But that is an interesting point. Thank you.'

'Glad to oblige, Miss. Are you all right, young sir?'

Orpheus had gone very still. 'I can smell it,' he muttered, gazing about.

'Smell what?' asked Rose, startled.

'Braxton's Baby Food!'

Rose sniffed the air. She turned to Buttercrumbe. 'Sir! You don't have children. Why would you have baby food?'

'Did you steal my sister from the orphanage?' Orpheus demanded.

'Orphanage?' Buttercrumbe sounded bewildered.

'Why are you using Braxton's baby food?' asked Rose again.

Buttercrumbe blinked. Then he chuckled. 'Come with me.'

He picked up a jar of glass eyes and led them into the back of the shop. Rose followed him with great caution. She crept past a fearsome bear rearing on its hind legs, and a number of birds of prey. Rose knew perfectly well they were inanimate objects but they still made the hairs rise on the back of her neck. Orpheus's fists were clenched.

They reached a small room where Mr Buttercrumbe did his taxidermy. The smell of baby food nearly knocked Rose over. Buttercrumbe picked up a jar of the stuff, and showed her a brush covered with it.

'I buy it in bulk to use as glue,' he explained. 'It works superbly in my trade. You see?'

He took the brush, and carefully painted a feather with it. Then he placed it on the wing of a half-preserved parrot.

Orpheus still looked suspicious but Rose leaned in to sniff the parrot. It did smell faintly of baby food.

'Glue,' she said, bemused.

'I may have to stop using it soon, however,' said Buttercrumbe. 'The price has gone up of late.'

'Has it?' said Rose.

'Yes. Rather annoying. Bit of a pennypincher, Dalrymple.'

They returned to the front of the shop, Rose deep in thought. The front door opened with the tinkle of a bell. Flinty the Forger eased inside, looking windblown. 'Buttercrumbe, old son?

Got a fine antique here. Genuine.' He held out a Roman-style helmet. Flecks of silver paint drifted from it. 'Forced to sell. Hard times. I'll take twenty guineas for it.'

'Flinty,' said Buttercrumbe sternly, 'We have discussed this before. No more fakery. I would sooner claim a chameleon to be a dragon than buy an item like this from you.'

'I happen to be a craftsman,' said Flinty, with dignity. 'I work with great respect for the artists of centuries past. If you wanted a nice replica of the Crown Jewels, sir, I'd whip 'em up for you in a jiffy.'

Rose's eyes widened. 'The Crown Jewels,' she murmured.

'What?' whispered Orpheus.

'Mr Flinty!' Rose rounded on him. 'Have you ever been asked to copy items from the Yorke Museum? Like a ruby vase?' She opened her locket and took out the glass jewel. 'Using these?'

'Uh, no, no, never,' Flinty stammered.

'A vase from the museum?' Buttercrumbe sounded disapproving. 'Just what have you been up to, Flinty?'

A whimper leaked from Flinty's throat. He edged towards the door.

'Flinty!' Rose blocked the way. 'Did you make a copy of the ruby vase?'

'Now, Miss, I wouldn't do that. 'Course not.'

'You just said you could copy the Crown Jewels!'

'Ah well, in a manner of speaking, like . . . '

'People know you make copies of valuable antiques,' snapped Orpheus.

Flinty hissed through his teeth. 'Here, keep a feller's business quiet!'

'I took a ruby from the vase in the Highborne to Locks and Clocks,' said Rose. 'It was a fake. Did you switch them over? And kill Angus Wood when he caught you in the act?'

'What?' Flinty yelped. He cringed away. 'I ain't no murderer. Never! I only did what I was paid for. Never set a foot in that hotel . . . '

'"Paid for"?' Orpheus cornered him. 'Someone paid you to make the fake? Who?'

Flinty sniffed. 'Don't know. Didn't ask the name.'

'Piffle!' Orpheus shouted. 'You're lying.'

'Better tell the truth, Flinty,' warned Buttercrumbe. 'It sounds like you're in this up to your neck.'

'You ain't the police.' Flinty hugged his Roman helmet. 'This is persecution, this is.'

'We could tell the police about that fake vase,' said Orpheus.

'No!' yelled Flinty.

'Well then?' said Rose.

'You can't protect the identity of a murderer!' said Orpheus.

Flinty pushed over the stuffed aardvark. Buttercrumbe cried out in dismay as the forger shoved past the children and bolted out the door.

Rose and Orpheus dashed out into the street in pursuit. It was snowing hard and the cobblestones were slippery with ice. Rose skidded and fell to her knees. Orpheus ran up against a fierce-looking matron who gave him the rough side of her tongue. Rose struggled to her feet, and peered desperately down the street but it was too late. Flinty had disappeared.

Chapter 12

A Creature of Wings and Claws

Orpheus lifted Rose to her feet. 'Rotten coward,' he panted. 'Flinty, I mean. Not you.'

Rose rubbed her knees. They were grazed, blood oozing through her stockings. 'Urgh. I wish the butlers had been with us. Bronson would have walloped him.'

'At least now we know he was involved,' said Orpheus. 'We know someone paid him to make the fake. I can't see Flinty as the murderer. I'd bet fifty pounds that the thief is the one who killed Wood.'

'Me too,' said Rose, catching her breath. 'We'd better tell the butlers. Maybe they've found some clue about Inaaya. Can I see that picture again?'

Orpheus took Inaaya's sketch from his pocket. 'The mystery bird,' he said. 'You know, I was looking at all the birds in Buttercrumbe's shop, just to see if there was anything that resembled it. I had also wondered if it was a peacock because of the dining room at the Highborne. But it doesn't look like a peacock, does it?'

Rose shook her head, thinking. 'Maybe it's an imaginary bird, like a phoenix. Mr Buttercrumbe could make a bird that looked like one, couldn't he? If he wanted to make a fake, like Flinty. Remember what he said about turning a chameleon into a dragon? He could do that, I'm sure. A dragon with scaly wings and claws!'

There was a long silence. Rose and Orpheus stared at the battered piece of paper.

'Oh no,' whispered Rose. 'Do you think—'

'I don't believe it,' groaned Orpheus. 'Why didn't we see it? Claws – ragged wings – but I never even thought of a—' He put his head in his hands. 'All this time we've followed the wrong clue!'

'I should have guessed earlier,' sighed Rose. 'I'm so sorry, Orpheus.'

'It's not your fault,' said Orpheus wearily. 'But where are we going to find dragons?'

'There are some carved into the cathedral,' said Rose, rubbing her temples. 'And there must be a dozen taverns with dragons in their names. We'll just have to investigate them all.'

They walked down the icy streets, shivering and despondent. Rose looked for anything resembling a dragon. Perhaps, she thought, Heddsworth would know of one.

Suddenly Orpheus sucked in a breath.

'What is it?' said Rose.

Orpheus pointed to a sign on a wall.

REWARD!
Missing Orphan

Boy aged about thirteen
Answers to the name Orpheus
Of Indian/Eastern appearance
Thick hair. Badly behaved
Two Guineas for safe return

BLEAKSTONE
ORPHANAGE

'Oh no,' whispered Rose.

Orpheus tore down the notice and stuffed it into his shirt. 'Two guineas?' he spluttered. That's more than two pounds! That could buy a dozen of your dresses – Agnes earns six pounds a year!'

'There will be other notices,' said Rose. 'And we don't know how many have seen them. With a reward like that, it will be all over Yorke. *Two guineas*! Let's go to the Stairs Below, quick!'

Orpheus nodded. Then he swivelled on his heel and pulled Rose back by the arm. 'Constable!' he hissed. 'Heading this way!'

'Don't run,' Rose warned him. 'Walk normally.'

Orpheus pulled his hat down over his hair. 'We've got to disguise me.'

'Maybe we could dress you as a girl,' said Rose, spotting her favourite shop, Fotheringay's Hat Emporium. 'In there. Now!'

'A *girl*?'

'Oh, for heaven's sake! You're more afraid of wearing a dress than being forced back to that orphanage?'

Dragging his heels, Orpheus followed her into the establishment. 'This is a ladies' shop!' he moaned.

The milliner, Miss Ada Fotheringay, was working on a massive hat crowned with green feathers. She gaped to see her visitors, and gaped even more when Rose explained what they required.

'I have a spare apron, Miss, but I don't have a second dress.'

'I can lend him a petticoat,' said Rose.

'I don't want a petticoat!' said Orpheus.

'We need a nice big hat, Miss Fotheringay, and he can wear my cloak. That should be enough until we get home.'

Miss Fotheringay led Rose behind a screen so she could remove a petticoat. By the time Rose emerged, Orpheus had been enveloped in the green feathery hat with a veil.

'Perfect!' said Rose.

Rose helped Orpheus into the petticoat. Then they tied the cloak over his shoulders. Rose giggled. Orpheus glared.

'Ah, he looks lovely!' said Miss Fotheringay. 'Is it for a costume ball, Miss Raventhorpe?'

'Er, something like that. We're much obliged,' said Rose. She paid for the hat, and they left the shop.

Feeling like fugitives, they hurried through the

snowy streets. 'We should still take the Stairs Below, just to be on the safe side,' said Rose.

'Good. I'm taking this hat off in there.'

'It suits you,' said Rose, grinning.

'Let's just find a door to the Stairs Below, all right?'

Rose found one. Her teeth chattered as she extracted her Infinity Key from her locket. Then they were in the dark passageway, and Orpheus was lighting a lantern.

They hurried through the winding maze. Rose was glad she had brought her rapier. It made her feel safer. All the same, she jumped when another lantern light appeared in the distance.

'Who's there?' a familiar voice called.

'Charlie Malone!' cried Rose and Orpheus in relief. 'It's us!'

The lantern-light bobbed as Charlie limped towards them. 'Grand to see you, er, ladies.' He grinned at Orpheus, who still held his hat.

'I know, very funny,' said Orpheus, looking at the flowery hat with loathing.

'What on earth is the costume for?' Charlie asked.

Rose explained. Charlie was instantly concerned. 'A two guinea reward? You need to go into hiding, Orpheus. Come back to the Hall with me. I was taking out special invitations for the Butlers' Ball.'

'How are preparations going?' asked Rose.

'Oh! Very well, apart from the fact we're missing two antique silver teaspoons. And that we're all worried to death about the murders, and the missing girls and the fact the Raven Society are sabotaging every fireplace in Yorke.'

They reached the imposing door to the Hall, and entered the grand ballroom. Two student butlers polished the parquet floor, watched by a critical Bronson. 'Soot everywhere,' one student groaned. 'Every time we clean it up, another sackful comes down the chimney.'

'No grumbling,' scolded Bronson. 'A butler keeps a stiff upper lip at all times.' She turned to the arrivals. 'Oh hello. Where is Heddsworth? And that terrible cousin of yours, Miss Raventhorpe?'

'Both at home,' said Rose. 'Heddsworth is trying to keep Bixby from taking over. He keeps polishing our silver and rearranging the table settings. And Herbert is working on the guest list for our supposed wedding. He still won't let go of the idea that we're engaged.'

'Oh dear,' said Charlie.

'Little horror,' said Bronson. 'I take it you want to see Miss Regemont? You two,' she added, turning to the students, 'I want an essay on the best way to remove soot from crystal, china, marble and silver. By tonight.'

Rose and her friends climbed the stairs to Miss Regemont's office. They found her wrapped up in a coat with three hot water bottles at her feet, polishing her rapier. 'Bracing weather,' she remarked. Her breath ghosted on the air. 'Hot tea, everyone?'

Fortified with tea, the butlers listened to Rose and Orpheus as they explained the latest events. They showed Inaaya's picture.

Bronson groaned. 'It does look like a dragon! How infuriating! And there must be so many around the city.'

'At least no one else has been murdered yet,' said Miss Regemont, gripping her teacup. 'I thought we had endured enough of that business last autumn. Now we have the butlers and Ravens at each other's throats. We must find out who killed those men.'

'I have an idea,' Rose ventured. 'I think I need to revisit the orphanage.'

Orpheus dropped his teacup on the table. 'You can't go back there,' he spluttered. 'Cornpepper's dangerous. And he was suspicious of you when you went there the first time. It's too risky!'

'We have to take risks, if we're going to find

Inaaya!' Rose argued back. 'I'm sure Cornpepper knows where she is. We have to get the truth out of him.'

'A few sharpeners might convince him,' said Charlie Malone, patting the hilt of his rapier. 'You should leave the questioning to us, Miss Raventhorpe. You're right about Cornpepper but we have to manage this carefully. There are children in that orphanage and we mustn't endanger them.'

'I can still talk to him,' Rose began to protest.

'No, Miss Raventhorpe!' Miss Regemont gave the girl her frostiest look. 'I commend your bravery but it is far better you allow us to question Cornpepper. We must—' She stopped. More sand came pouring down the chimney.

'Not again!' Bronson drew her rapier.

There were shouts from outside the door, and a wild-eyed young butler ran in. 'Madam, there are sweeps on the roof! They're fighting the butlers on patrol!'

Miss Regemont leaped to her feet. The three younger butlers rushed from the room.

'Go home, you two,' Miss Regemont ordered the children. 'We are under siege. Out!'

Back in the Stairs Below, Rose and Orpheus argued by the light of their lantern.

'We should have stayed and fought with them,' Orpheus repeated. 'I don't care what Regemont said – they need our help!'

'Ordinarily I would,' Rose shot back. 'I'm a Raventhorpe and a Guardian of Yorke! But don't you see? This is our chance to go to Cornpepper. We have to do it now. Time is of the essence, Orpheus. You want to find Inaaya? We have to get the truth out of him.'

Orpheus kicked at a pebble. 'Fine. Tell me what we're going to do. I suppose you have it all planned out.'

'I do,' said Rose. 'You go home now, as fast as possible. I will go to Bleakstone as an orphan, sent by the parish. Once Cornpepper lets me in, I will question the orphans about Inaaya and her disappearance. After a few hours you can send Heddsworth to come and say it was a mistake, and he can take me out again.'

'Are you mad?' Orpheus's voice echoed off the walls. 'You just stroll into the Muckyards? And what if Cornpepper doesn't let you out again?'

'He will,' said Rose stubbornly. 'It's an orphanage, not a prison. And I'll take the Stairs Below most of the way. I'll be disguised. No one should bother me.'

'Why aren't we telling Heddsworth all this first?'

'Because he wouldn't let me do it,' Rose snapped. 'And if he did, Mother might find out and then she would have a good reason to sack him. He can scold me later. This is the fastest way to find out what we need to know.'

'Cornpepper might recognise you from when you visited before.'

'Not if I'm in disguise,' said Rose. 'I'll buy some suitable clothes at a stall.'

'I don't like it.' Orpheus scowled down at his lantern. 'You don't know what Cornpepper's like. You won't be able to take your rapier.'

'I'll be fine,' said Rose. 'Here, take it home for me. We're going to find Inaaya, Orpheus. I can feel it.'

Chapter 13

THE DRAGON-HILTED SWORD

Cornpepper stared at the frowzy girl on his doorstep. Rose wore a maid's old clothes, with her hair hidden under an unbecoming maid's cap.

'I've no family left, sir,' said Rose humbly. 'And the parish folks said you'd look after me.'

'We're full up,' said Cornpepper.

'I understand, sir. I don't suppose I have enough money to pay for my keep.'

Cornpepper perked up. 'Brass? How much?'

'Oh, not very much. I've barely a pound, sir.'

Cornpepper grabbed Rose by the arm. 'We'll find room,' he said. 'We'll treat you like royalty.'

He snatched the money Rose produced and dragged her down the corridor towards a dormitory. His dog, Lucifer, set up a cacophony of barks.

'Shut it,' said Cornpepper. He turned to Rose. 'Don't mess with the dog, right? I got to enter you in the register. Get your particulars. Name? How old're you?'

'Rose. I'm twelve,' said Rose.

'Hmm,' said Cornpepper. 'Old enough to work then. I'll find somewhere to send you, and then you'll be out of here.'

He pushed a door open, and Rose saw a line of grey beds, and ragged children huddled in a corner.

'Off with that cap,' said Cornpepper. 'Let's have a proper look at you.'

Rose obeyed. Cornpepper inspected her like a pig at the market.

'Nice hair for a pauper brat,' he observed. 'Should

fetch a good price, for them that buy false hairpieces. We'll have to cut it all off.'

'What?' squeaked Rose.

'Scissors!' shouted Cornpepper. 'Where'd I put the things?'

Rose put her hands over her head, stricken. It was shameful vanity, but she didn't want to lose her hair.

Cornpepper marched out. Rose looked miserably at the other orphans, watching her from the corner.

'Try not to think about it,' advised one girl. Rose remembered her from last time. Corrie.

'Look, I'm here to find out what happened to Orpheus's sister Inaaya,' Rose whispered.

The orphans exchanged fearful glances. 'We don't know,' one replied. 'She just vanished.'

'She didn't tell you anything? Nothing suspicious?'

They shook their heads.

Rose chewed her lip. 'I'll have to search Cornpepper's office,' she muttered.

The orphans gasped. 'You can't do that!' one whispered. 'What about the dog?'

'Perhaps someone could create a diversion,' Rose suggested. Instantly she regretted the words. She couldn't ask the orphans to get into trouble for her.

'We can get Lucifer away,' said one girl thoughtfully. 'He likes gingerbread.'

'Gingerbread? Really?'

'We have some hidden away for emergencies.' The girl went to a window ledge, felt underneath it, and brought out a battered tin box. She opened it and hid a piece of gingerbread in her hand.

Lucifer padded in, growling softly.

There was the sound of gingerbread hitting the floor. Lucifer darted towards it.

Rose scurried out.

Perspiring with nerves, she tiptoed to the office. There was, thankfully, no sign of Cornpepper. She opened the ledgers and dusty books on the desk, scanning figures and names and columns. The records were surprisingly neat, and properly spelled. She read:

Orphan: Lotty Birch. Aged 7 years. Died: May 8, typhus. Burial arranged.

Orphan: Stanley Smith. Aged 8 years. Died October 4, convulsions. Buried in pauper's grave.

Beneath these records was a letter, dated a few days ago:

December 19

Dear Reverend Bailey,

Thank you for your esteemed benevolence in providing for our orphans. I assure you that the foundling child you sent us, Lotty Birch, is thriving and will do well as a maid in future. Your continued payment for her welfare is much appreciated.

Yours obediently,
Jabez Cornpepper

Rose heard footsteps. Panicking, she seized the records book and ducked behind the door.

Cornpepper entered, muttering, and pulled a pair of scissors from his desk drawer. Rose wondered how long it would take for him to notice the missing book. If she was fast, she could run back to the dormitory and . . .

She stopped. There was something leaning against the desk.

A dragon-hilted sword.

Rose's heartbeat thundered in her chest. Could it belong to Cornpepper? She couldn't believe it did. Had he stolen it, then? This had to be the reason Inaaya had drawn a dragon.

Rose heard the patter of paws on the flagstones. Lucifer entered, sniffed, and started growling.

'Lucifer! Come here!'

Lucifer's hackles were up. He snarled at Rose, who held the book tightly to her chest like armour.

Cornpepper turned round, and stared directly

at her. He blinked, turning scarlet with fury and astonishment. Rose swallowed hard.

'You thievin' little brat! Gimme that book. You can go to solitary!'

Rose fought like a cat but Cornpepper had an iron grip and took the book from her easily. The dog barked, snarling and snapping at Rose's legs. Cornpepper snatched up her long dark braid. The scissors were cold against the nape of her neck. *Snick.*

Rose stared open-mouthed as Cornpepper dropped her braid on to the desk. She put a hand to her hair, which now fell in short uneven strands about her face.

She was dragged up a flight of stairs, then another. Cornpepper dug a key out from his pocket. He unlocked the door, and shoved Rose into the room. The door slammed shut behind him.

As Rose slumped on the floor in despair, she heard a voice croak in the darkness.

'*Miss Raventhorpe?*'

*

Agnes the maid rushed into the kitchen. 'Begging your pardon, Orpheus,' she said, 'but Miss Rose sent you a message. Urgent-like. She needs help.'

Orpheus groaned. 'I knew it! I haven't even had a chance to talk to Heddsworth! When he comes back from his errands, tell him I've gone to the orphanage on Gigg Street. Tell him to meet me at Bleakstone.'

Orpheus sped downstairs and slipped out the back door, throwing a cloak over his usual clothes. The wind blew him halfway to Cathedral Green. Would it never stop storming, stop snowing?

The cathedral looked peaceful under its snow blanket. Orpheus gulped a mouthful of snowflakes. He needed courage. The thought of returning to Gigg Street, the Muckyards, made his stomach curdle.

Rose needed him.

He forced his legs across the Green. The paths had been cleared but fresh snow piled up relentlessly.

He wished Rose had given him her Infinity Key. The Stairs Below would have come in useful just now.

Slowly, stubbornly, he made his way to Gigg Street. Then down the narrow, winding skitterways that led towards Bleakstone Orphanage. In his mind, Orpheus scolded Rose. *Did you really think this would work? Why couldn't you let the butlers help you?*

He ventured further down the street. Christmas cheer was thin in this part of the city. No beribboned wreaths hung here. He was getting close to Bleakstone—

Someone took him by the arm.

'Hello there, brat,' said a voice in his ear.

Orpheus gulped.

It was Cornpepper.

Orpheus opened his mouth to shout for help, only to feel the tip of a knife at his back. 'No,' said Cornpepper. 'No squeakin'. We'll be civil-like, now.'

'You see?' said another voice. 'I told you he'd come.'

And Herbert stepped out of the shadows, the picture of smug triumph.

Chapter 14

A Kidnapped Accomplice

Orpheus couldn't believe he'd fallen for such an obvious trick.

'You did this,' he choked out, glaring at Herbert. 'You gave Agnes a fake message!'

'Thought you were smarter than me, didn't you, street urchin?' mocked Herbert. 'But it was so easy! Now I get to pocket the reward, and you go back to the orphanage, where you belong.'

Cornpepper pressed the knife closer to Orpheus's back and clapped his hand over the boy's mouth for good measure. 'Come on,' he grunted to Herbert. 'No reward 'til he's back in Bleakstone.'

Cornpepper forced Orpheus up the orphanage steps. Orpheus tried to think of some way to warn Herbert. If just one of them could escape!

He was dragged inside. Cornpepper grinned his unpleasant grin. 'Welcome back,' he said. 'Our little lost lamb.'

'My reward,' said Herbert, holding out his hand.

Cornpepper grabbed the young man by the scruff of his neck and pulled him forward. 'Oh, I don't think so.'

'What?' sputtered Herbert.

'Hmm,' said Cornpepper, eyeing Herbert's fine clothes. 'Might be able to sell them threads for a shillin' or two.'

'How dare you!' Herbert kicked at him ferociously. 'I am the future Earl of Dundragan!'

Lucifer the dog came trotting up, snarling. Herbert cowered. The two boys were dragged past wide-eyed orphans, down a set of stairs, and into the cellar. The door slammed shut behind them and they heard the snick of a lock.

Orpheus waited until Herbert had got all the shouting out of his system. 'I'm a Dundragan! I'll have you all arrested! This is an *outrage!*'

'Congratulations,' snapped Orpheus. 'Now we're both stuck in this mess.'

Herbert kicked the door. 'But what are they going to do?' he demanded fearfully.

'Well, they're not going to throw us a party with strawberry tarts.' Orpheus closed his eyes. At least he wasn't alone, he told himself. Even Herbert was better than nobody. 'I hope Rose got out of here in one piece.'

'They can't leave us in here!'

'They can,' said Orpheus. 'They can kill us and ditch our bodies and nobody'll know.'

'You're trying to scare me,' said Herbert. His voice was high and uncertain.

'I'm not the one who just sold us both to Cornpepper!' As soon as he said it, Orpheus regretted his outburst. It wasn't helping anyone.

Herbert was silent for a minute. At last he said sulkily, 'There must be a way out.'

Orpheus went to the door and listened. He heard the grumbling of Cornpepper, and the snuffling breath of the dog. The click of claws on the floor. The whimpers of cowed children.

He felt in his pockets.

'Hey!' he whispered. 'I've got a pocket knife in here. Cornpepper didn't search me!'

In the darkness he heard Herbert search his own pockets. 'I've nothing much,' Herbert grumbled. 'Have you any food?'

'No.' Orpheus gingerly inserted the knife in the lock. The lock refused to budge.

He sank back despondently.

'I hope they take us to wherever my sister is. If she's still alive.'

They waited in the darkness for a long time. Long enough to feel thoroughly miserable, thirsty, hungry and scared. Orpheus wondered which of them would die first. Then he decided to stop thinking like that.

Footsteps approached the cellar.

A key turned in the lock. The boys scrambled to their feet. The door opened.

Orpheus gaped. It was the last person he had expected to see.

Rose heard an intake of breath, and the rustle of someone sitting up. She squinted into the darkness.

'Garnet!' Rose gasped. 'Garnet Goldsmith!'

As her eyes adjusted to the dimness, Rose noticed her friend's thin cheeks and dirty dress.

'What are you doing here, Miss Raventhorpe?' stammered Garnet.

'I got into a spot of trouble,' said Rose. She touched her shorn head where her braid had once been.

Garnet stared at her, eyes alight with hope. 'Are your butler friends coming to rescue you?'

'They don't know I'm here,' confessed Rose, ashamed. 'Are you all right? How long have you been here?'

'Weeks,' said Garnet, her voice shaking. 'Is my father all right? Have you seen him?'

'He looks terribly tired and worn out. What happened, Garnet?'

'I'll tell you what happened,' said Garnet bitterly. 'I was a fool.' She scrunched the folds of her dress in her fingers. 'A few weeks ago Flinty the Forger came into the shop, and asked me if I was a jeweller. He'd heard rumours that I was as good as Father. I should have turned him out, but I was curious about what he wanted.

'He showed me a picture of a beautiful ruby-studded vase, and told me he'd been asked to make a copy of it. For a customer, he said, just for insurance purposes, all perfectly legal. But he wasn't highly skilled at copying jewels. He didn't have the right glass gems. He needed my help, if I was willing to take a fee and keep quiet about it. I didn't believe it was legitimate, Rose. Not for one minute.'

Rose took her hand.

'I can guess what happened,' she said gently. 'You agreed, didn't you?'

Tears rolled down Garnet's face.

180

'I shouldn't have done it, Rose. But I was so angry with Father not telling people about my work! He thinks girls shouldn't work as professional jewellers. So I did it. I gave him the false gems. Flinty paid me and left.

'Then I heard there were special museum pieces on display at the Highborne. One was a ruby vase. I guessed then what he'd done. What I'd done! Someone wanted to steal that vase. I was so ashamed, Rose. I couldn't bear to tell Father or the police. But I went and found Flinty, to tell him to give back those gems or I'd confess everything.

'The next day, I went out on an errand for Father, and a man grabbed me and threw me into a carriage. He pointed a pistol at me! And he brought me here. I've been in this room ever since. That Cornpepper said my father would have to pay a huge ransom for me or I'd go to prison for forgery. Or worse. It's more money than Father has, Rose. I don't know what to do!'

Rose hugged her. 'Garnet, it's all right. We'll get out of here.'

'Father will hate me for this.'

'He will not. He's terribly worried. He's been saying you're ill, but I knew you weren't. I have your bracelet, back at home. Why did you take it off?'

'I couldn't bear to wear it anymore, not after what I did,' said Garnet.

Some straw rustled in the dim room. Garnet turned her head.

With shock, Rose realised there was another person in the room.

'She's woken up,' said Garnet. She scurried over to the corner to stroke the person's hair and whisper to her.

The girl pushed aside a ragged blanket, sat up, and stared at Rose. She had roughly cut hair, and she was terribly thin. But her resemblance to Orpheus was unmistakable.

Inaaya.

Chapter 15

A Bleak House

'Who are you?' Inaaya asked, blinking at Rose. She reached for Garnet's hand.

'It's all right,' Garnet soothed. 'She's a friend. Miss Rose Raventhorpe.'

'I'm friends with Orpheus,' said Rose gently. 'We've been looking for you.'

'Orpheus!' Inaaya looked frantic. 'Is he here? Is he all right?'

'He's well, but he's trying to find you,' explained Rose. 'Have you been here all this time? What happened?'

Inaaya gulped. 'It was all because I wouldn't eat that horrible green food! Half the orphans were getting sick from it. But they kept eating it because they were hungry. I heard the Dragon Man talking to Cornpepper about it. Saying we had to test it for him. I don't know the Dragon Man's name. I only saw his sword.'

'I wanted to warn Orpheus about him, if he came back. So I drew a picture of a dragon, and hid it under my bed. That's how we used to leave messages for each other. But after I hid the picture, Cornpepper came to put me in solitary. He said I was the only orphan not eating that food and I needed to learn a lesson. Then he brought Garnet up here too.'

Garnet gave her hand a grateful squeeze. 'At least we've kept each other company.'

Rose looked at the door.

'I've tried breaking the lock,' said Garnet. 'But I can't. And that window's too high up.'

'Who brings your food? Who empties the chamberpot?'

'Cornpepper,' said Inaaya. 'And he always has the dog with him.' She smiled faintly. 'Lucifer brings dog bones sometimes and leaves them behind. Sometimes we chew on them, rather than the awful green stuff.'

'Oh Garnet,' said Rose. She wished she had some food for them. Then she wondered how long it would be before she was also chewing on dog bones.

'Is there any way we can get past the dog? Is it scared of anything?'

'Scared of anything?' said Garnet, incredulous. 'That dog?'

'Yes he is,' said Inaaya unexpectedly.

They both turned to look at her. 'Thunder,' she explained. 'And fire. He whines and cries when it's stormy.'

'Well, we can't organise a thunderstorm,' said Rose. 'And there's no fire in here. It's freezing!'

She looked around the tiny room. She ran her fingers over traces of gilt wallpaper, and a monogram. She stared at it so long that Garnet frowned. 'What are you doing?'

Rose was muttering under her breath. 'Oh, Saint Iphigenia's cats,' she said aloud. 'I think I know who used to own this place.'

Orpheus stared at the pink-cheeked young woman standing in the doorway to the cellar with Lucifer the dog.

'Miss Caroline?' he stammered. 'What are you doing here?'

Caroline sighed. 'You again! Jabez told me that some rich boy was bringing an escaped orphan back here.'

'What do you mean?' Orpheus felt sick. This was no rescue.

'Jabez convinced me we could make more money out of both of you but I had to be sure he didn't make a mess of it,' said Caroline. 'He's not terribly bright, I'm afraid.'

Orpheus still didn't understand. 'Why – why

would you be working with Cornpepper?' he asked. 'How could you have any connection to this horrible old orphanage?'

Caroline Chippingdale's doll–like face turned a violent red. 'Because Bleakstone is MY HOUSE! The Chippingdale mansion. And it's full of horrible, noisy, smelly, dirty children!'

'*Your* house? How can this be your house?' sputtered Orpheus.

Caroline pulled fastidiously at the fingers of her glove. 'Bleakstone was our family home,' she said. Her eyes lit up, reliving some distant memory. 'It had velvet curtains, gilt mirrors and a conservatory! I used to have flowers in my room every day! And we had servants who kept their place. Then our parents died, leaving us with huge debts, and *nothing* to support us. Jabez has had to take a false name, of course. A Chippingdale cannot run an orphanage! I must say, despite being so lack–witted, he can play the part of a commoner very well.'

'Cornpepper is your brother?' asked Herbert, puzzled. 'That nasty creature who kidnapped us?'

'Yes,' snapped Caroline. 'We had to sell our house – our beautiful Bleakstone – but when we were old enough, Jabez pretended to be a clergyman who wanted to care for children. He managed to convince the orphanage committee that he could run it. Most of his wages come to me, so at least one of us can live as a Chippingdale ought.'

Orpheus was still struggling to comprehend it all. 'You're an orphan too. Don't you care what your brother does to these children?'

She glared at him. 'It's about having our home and our position in society back. Don't you understand that? Wouldn't you do anything to get your home back, once you'd lost it?'

'But,' Orpheus croaked, 'where will the orphans go? This is the only home they have!'

'They don't want to be here!' Caroline wrinkled her nose. 'Once I have enough money, I can restore

Bleakstone to its former glory. Then they can work as servants or shovel snow. I will have brocade sofas in the parlour, and ferns in Grecian urns, and a piano. I shall find someone rich to marry. And we will be wealthy again.'

Orpheus stared at her. Then he went to the wall and leaned back on it, resting a foot squarely on the peeling wallpaper.

Caroline's face turned a darker shade of raspberry.

'Get your filthy foot off my wall.'

'What, this foot?' said Orpheus. 'I don't think so.'

'Get it off! Take it off this minute!'

'My boot's very dirty,' said Orpheus. 'I've been trudging through the streets. Plenty of dog and horse droppings, old vegetables on my boots.'

Herbert kicked the wall. 'Shabby old place, I agree,' he said loudly. 'Disgraceful.'

It was too much for Caroline. She flew at them, shrieking. Lucifer barked, trapped behind Caroline's skirts.

The boys made a run for it. They crashed out of the doorway.

Rose jumped as a key jiggled in the lock. She prayed that Heddsworth had come to the rescue. But when the door opened, Cornpepper stood there, holding the dragon-hilted sword.

'Jeweller's girl,' he snapped. 'Your pa has come. He brought a sackful of money, and you're to go free.'

'Oh!' Garnet wobbled to her feet.

'Hurry up.'

'W ... what about them?' Garnet gestured to Rose and Inaaya.

'They stay here.' Cornpepper smirked.

Garnet gave them a despairing look.

'Is that what Caroline wants?' Rose asked Cornpepper suddenly.

Cornpepper looked like scalded milk.

'What?'

'Caroline,' said Rose. 'There's writing on the

wallpaper here. "Caroline Chippingdale". This
house belonged to her once, didn't it?'

'Not just her! Both of us!' Cornpepper snapped.
Suddenly his common accent disappeared, and he
was an arrogant young gentleman like Herbert.
'I've been slaving here while she swans around
playing the lady! Just because I'm not a pretty face
like her. She'd better make it worth my while. I've
had to spend years of my life in this place, playing
nursemaid to common, baseborn brats!'

'You're Caroline's brother? The one who is
supposed to be abroad?' Rose scrutinised his
features. 'I should have noticed the resemblance.
You have the same chin.'

'She doesn't have a pox-scarred face like me,'
grumbled Cornpepper. 'So she can attract a rich
man. I'm the one who has to play the scabby
commoner and deal with snotty little runts all day.'

'You don't look after them,' said Rose in disgust.
'I saw those records. You give them terrible food,
let children die and lie about it to the authorities.

You take money for their upkeep even when they're dead. You're an Angelmaker!'

Cornpepper – Jabez Chippingdale – grew pinched at the mouth. 'I'm burning those records and then I'm going to get the Dragon Man to deal with you.'

'Who is—'

Jabez seized Garnet by the wrist. 'Come on, you're out. And keep silent, or you'll pay for it.'

'What is going on here, Master Jabez?'

Another face appeared in the doorway. He looked hot and irritated. Rose opened her mouth to speak, but nothing came out.

Henry Dalrymple.

Chapter 16

Fear and Flame

The three girls stared up at Dalrymple. Rose felt a rush of hope. Could Dalrymple be here to help them?

'Mr Dalrymple! Cornpepper is an Angelmaker! He lets children die, and takes money for them. He buys your baby food . . . ' Her voice tailed off. Inaaya was trembling beside her.

Dalrymple took the dragon-hilted rapier from Jabez.

'Master Jabez?' Dalrymple sighed. 'Did you really

need to borrow my rapier again? Lucifer should be all you need to keep the dashed little brats quiet. I would rather keep the blade for my own protection.'

'They're wily, Dalrymple,' Jabez Chippingdale muttered. 'Wily little horrors, and Caroline took Lucifer with her.'

Rose heard someone else run upstairs. Caroline Chippingdale rushed into view. 'Those wretched boys escaped!' she cried. 'The orphan brats distracted Lucifer. You must go and stop them, Dalrymple!'

'For pity's sake, Miss Caroline,' growled Dalrymple, 'How many children are loose here? Send Master Jabez down.'

'I'm sick of doing this dirty work,' said Jabez sulkily. 'I'll lock the girls up again, Dalrymple can sort it out.'

'Oh, do as you're told, Jabez!' snapped Caroline.

Rose felt completely bewildered. 'Mr Dalrymple is in league with both of you? Why would he want to help you?'

Caroline sniffed. 'You have a butler yourself, Miss Raventhorpe. I am surprised you couldn't see it. Dalrymple was our family butler. When our parents died, he promised unswerving loyalty to the Chippingdales. And that he would do whatever was necessary to restore our fortunes. And he will be suitably rewarded once we have our home and our position in society back.'

'I will be very glad to return to my proper duties, Miss Caroline,' said Dalrymple. 'Working as a factory owner is not my strong suit.' He shuddered. 'Disgusting place. The smells! The commonness of it all!' He held out his fingers. 'I long to put on white gloves again. I am a butler to the core.'

'A *butler*?' Rose gaped at him. 'The Chippingdale family butler?'

'Indeed.' Caroline tipped her chin high. 'He spent his savings on that decaying old factory, and has raised nearly enough money to buy back Bleakstone. Jabez sent him orphans to work there for free, and they were also useful for testing new products. Added to what I've made on that vase, we will be a grand family again, grander than you Raventhorpes! We will own land, and London houses, and I will marry whoever I fancy.'

'And I will be a butler again, a better butler than that posturing Mayfair,' sneered Dalrymple. 'He didn't like being suspected of murder, oh no! I sent a box of gingerbread to him, to give him a fright. Served him right.'

'Dalrymple murdered the sweep at the Highborne,' Rose suddenly realised. 'Then you returned to the parlour while Caroline switched the vase! And you gave each other alibis . . . '

'I kept an eye on that sweep,' growled Dalrymple. 'Told him to mind his own business while we were there. But he decided to stickybeak, and Miss Caroline had me deal with him.'

'The ruby vase made a good weapon,' Caroline agreed. 'A good, heavy weapon.'

'Your hatbox,' said Rose, in a flash of realisation.

'You put the real vase in your hatbox after you switched it with the fake!'

'Under a real hat, just in case anyone looked,' said Caroline smugly. 'That vase fetched a fortune! I am grateful you helped to make a good copy, Miss Goldsmith. A pity you didn't want to keep your mouth shut. Flinty told me you were starting to waver. So poor Dalrymple had to disguise himself and kidnap you. It would have been easier to silence you altogether but the money from your father will help to make us rich again.'

'I was foolish,' said Garnet in disgust. 'But you're insane.'

Dalrymple stepped forward, cracking his finger joints. 'Do not speak like that to Miss Caroline!'

'So you murdered Mayfair too?' Rose demanded. 'Why? What had he done?'

'Mayfair refused to sell Braxton Foods products in the hotel,' said Caroline loftily. 'He sent Dalrymple a vile, dismissive letter. He said they didn't meet hotel standards!'

'And I showed him,' said Dalrymple, with a grisly smile. 'Miss Caroline said it was a good idea to make the sweeps look like they'd done it. Easy as a wink. Poker to the head.'

Rose turned to Jabez, who was watching his sister with a mixture of admiration and resentment.

'So Jabez was in this too. Playing a role.'

'He did what he was told,' sneered Caroline. 'It's not as if he was much use at restoring the family fortunes. No looks or wits to speak of!'

Jabez touched his pitted face. 'When we have money again, I can make a good match too,' he muttered.

'You couldn't marry,' said Caroline, with scorn. 'Not with your face! No woman would want you. At least I stand a decent chance in the marriage market!'

Jabez glowered. 'I've done more than enough for our family,' he grumbled.

'You have kept an eye on our home, at least,' sniffed Caroline. 'We will have Bleakstone again.'

'Not if I have anything to do with it!' Rose trembled with outrage. 'Jabez is an Angelmaker, letting orphans die and taking money for them. You're a thief and a kidnapper, and Dalrymple is a murderer.'

Dalrymple took another step forward.

'You forget, Miss,' he growled. 'I'm a butler of Yorke. I know how to fight.' He lifted his dragon-hilted blade.

'You studied at the Hall?' Rose couldn't believe it. 'The butlers would have remembered you! Recognised you!'

'A student butler who was expelled for making inferior cucumber sandwiches?' Dalrymple rolled his eyes. 'Why would they? I was nothing to them. I found employment with the Chippingdales and they were better to me than Silvercrest Hall ever was! Why would the butlers pay attention to a mere factory owner?' He pointed the blade at Rose's throat.

'Leave her alone!' shouted a voice from the stairwell.

It was Orpheus. Herbert was a few steps behind him.

'Orpheus!' shrieked Inaaya. She threw herself past Dalrymple to embrace her brother. Orpheus hugged his sister tightly.

'Lock them all up, Dalrymple,' ordered Caroline. 'We'll get rid of them one way or another.'

Lucifer came bounding upstairs, growling at the intruders. He darted forward, knocking Dalrymple off balance. There was a confused struggle as Jabez seized Garnet, Caroline grabbed Rose, and Dalrymple lunged for Orpheus and Inaaya.

'I smell smoke!' yelped Herbert.

Rose had been busy stamping on Caroline's toes. 'Fire?'

That caught Caroline's attention. She looked past Rose to see black smoke rolling up the stairs.

'No!' Caroline screamed. She turned on her brother. 'Jabez! This is your fault! I told you and told you not to let those brats damage our house!'

'It isn't my fault,' her brother whined. 'It's the chimney. I wanted to call for a sweep, but you said to wait because sweeps cost money!'

'Run!' cried Dalrymple.

There was a sudden rush down the stairs, a swish of skirts, and the terrified whimpering of Lucifer, who was left behind. Caroline, her brother, and their butler had bolted downstairs.

'Come on!' Orpheus beckoned frantically to the girls. 'Hurry! They'll have left the orphans!' He stopped to gape at Rose's cropped head. 'Your hair. He cut your hair.'

'Rose, you look terrible!' scolded Herbert. 'I can't marry you looking like that. You'd better grow it out.'

'You're worried about my hair? What are you even doing here, Herbert?'

'He tricked me,' said Orpheus. 'And got kidnapped as well. I didn't have time to tell Heddsworth anything. Come on, downstairs!'

Rose seized Garnet's hand. Lucifer whined

against her skirt. They all pulled their clothing over their mouths against the smoke. Already their eyes were stinging. It was hard to breathe.

As they ran downstairs, Rose could hear the news spreading out in the street. There were cries of 'fire!' and a rush of panicked feet. Then they saw a group of terrified orphans rushing up the stairs to meet them.

'We can't get out,' cried Corrie. 'They've locked us in!'

'Back upstairs,' coughed Rose. 'There might be a window we can use.'

The children streamed upstairs, some coughing, some crying, some trying to calm the others. Lucifer followed them, scrambling, his tail between his legs.

'The attic,' said Rose. 'We'll go to the roof!'

'There's a trapdoor,' said Corrie. 'We're not supposed to know about it.'

To everyone's great relief, when they reached it, the trapdoor was not locked. The children struggled to help each other up one by one. Lucifer whined and howled, so with great difficulty they pulled him up behind them.

Orpheus and Rose were searching for an escape route from the roof.

'I could risk the jump,' said Orpheus, eyeing a five-foot leap to the next building.

'You can't!' Rose looked at the drop to the cobblestones. 'We need a plank, something that can serve as a bridge.'

People were gathering on the street below, trying to douse the flames. Rose shouted and waved to attract their attention. She saw upturned faces. People pointed and ran, returning with mattresses and stretchers. None would help much if they had to jump off a three-storey building.

But the fire had taken hold, roaring and crackling its way up the building, and Rose feared the roof would soon collapse. The children held hands, shaking with terror.

Rose saw someone moving through the smoke.

People on the neighbouring rooftop. She grabbed Orpheus's arm and pointed.

The moving figures drew closer. Rose squinted. They were darkly clad, and moved swiftly.

Fawney and the sweeps.

They had a ladder! The Ravens pushed it across the gap between the buildings, and beckoned the children over. Everyone rushed over. They gazed fearfully downwards.

'Keep your weight on the end,' shouted Fawney to Orpheus. 'Let the little ones climb over first!'

'They're scared!' Rose shouted back.

'I'll go,' said one boy bravely.

Rose prayed the ladder was strong enough. That the boy didn't grow dizzy and fall. She and Orpheus sat on the end of the ladder and watched as the boy crawled carefully on to the bars.

Rose counted under her breath as, rung by rung, he inched across the gap. The seconds felt very long to her, but soon the sweeps were holding out their arms and pulling the boy across the last few feet to safety.

Then the other children had to be coaxed across. Having seen their friend make it safely, more were willing to try. But several clung to Rose and Orpheus.

'We can't cross all at once,' said Orpheus. 'The ladder'll break.'

The clamour below grew louder. Firefighters had arrived, and were attacking the blaze. Herbert kept saying he should go across next, but Rose fiercely told him to wait. One of the smaller children was still making her way across. The sweeps shouted at them to hurry.

And then the ladder broke.

Chapter 17

CATS AND RAVENS

The girl who was on the ladder only just made it to the other rooftop, dragged to safety by the sweeps. The children watched in horror as the broken ladder crashed to the ground in pieces.

Rose stared across the gap. As the chimney sweeps waved and gestured, Rose heard the crackle of fire behind them. She turned round. Flames were shooting out of the trapdoor.

The sweeps brought another ladder. They pushed it carefully across the gap. There were still a dozen children needing rescue.

Orpheus and Rose encouraged each child over the ladder. It was a long process, every child frightened, and everyone afraid that one would slip and fall. Inaaya clung to Orpheus on the roof, and he had to encourage her in Hindi before she would venture on the ladder.

Garnet took Inaaya's hand. Herbert whimpered. Then Rose and Orpheus were pushing and leading the children up the ladder, as the roof behind them began to collapse.

Orpheus seized Lucifer, and somehow they got the frightened dog across the ladder.

Fawney pulled them all to safety on the neighbouring roof.

'Downstairs!' he shouted. 'Quickly!'

The sweeps lifted the smallest children into their arms, and led the rest into an attic and down flight after flight of stairs. The building seemed to be an office, quiet and unused, but Rose was too exhausted to pay much attention. The sweeps eventually brought them outside, and the group gathered together in a shocked and shivering bunch.

Herbert collapsed on the snow. 'I'm never leaving the ground again,' he wheezed. 'Ever.'

They looked up at the glow of the fire.

Through the smoke and heat, Rose thought she saw the cat statues of Yorke, moving. She screwed up her eyes, and glimpsed a black cat that looked like Watchful dashing across the rooftops. The other cats came running to join him, crossing gutters and leaping from chimneys.

Rose felt cool, light touches on her face. Snowflakes.

As the crowd watched, the snow spun into a sharp whirlwind. Cold rushed through Rose. Giant white flakes fell on to the fiery, glowing remains of Bleakstone Orphanage, dousing the embers and sparks that threatened the neighbouring buildings and the city itself.

The fire was going out.

Rose blinked away the smoke, and saw the cats were no longer visible. Their work here was finished.

Everyone huddled together. Then they saw Heddsworth, Charlie Malone and Bronson pelting towards them. They were smoke-smudged and dishevelled, far from their usual immaculate selves.

'Saint Iphigenia's CATS!' shouted Bronson. 'We thought you were all . . . We nearly . . . Are you all right?'

Heddsworth had his medical kit at the ready. 'Are you hurt? Burned?' The butlers went from one child to the next. 'We saw the fire from the rooftop of the Hall,' Charlie Malone explained. 'The sweeps suddenly took off across the rooftops. We could barely keep up with them.'

'We're fine, I think,' said Rose. Her voice was raspy from all the smoke.

'Your hair!' said Charlie Malone. 'What happened? Was it burned?'

'Someone cut it off,' said Rose. 'It doesn't matter.'

Heddsworth turned to Orpheus and his sister. 'Is this Miss Inaaya? Delighted to meet you, young lady. Glad to see you safe and well. Miss Raventhorpe, the next time you do anything like this, without telling me, I shall inform your father myself.'

'The orphans can stay at the Hall tonight,' said Bronson, giving a child a drink of water. 'We shall have the chimneys cleared and fires lit in no time.'

'Garnet!' someone shouted.

Garnet let out a cry. Her father, Mr Goldsmith, ran towards her and swept his daughter into his arms. Rose watched happily. She must remember to return Garnet's bracelet to her.

Then she became aware of a commotion.

Caroline and Jabez stood before the ruin of Bleakstone, shouting at each other. 'Look what you've done!' yelled Caroline. 'Our house is in ruins!'

'It's not my fault!' Jabez bellowed back. 'And where's the money you've raised for us? Or have you spent it all on fancy dresses? It's my turn to live like a Chippingdale!'

Dalrymple tried to hold them apart. 'Miss Caroline! Master Jabez!'

'What is that all about?' Charlie Malone stared at the group.

'They're in league,' Rose explained. 'Dalrymple is the Chippingdale butler. He committed the murders so Caroline and Jabez Chippingdale could recover their fortunes.'

'Dalrymple?' Heddsworth turned to her sharply. 'A butler?'

'He was expelled from the Hall as a student,' said Rose, wiping soot streaks off her face.

'I remember now!' exclaimed Charlie Malone. 'Miss Regemont told us about expelling a student once for poor work. That was him?'

Heddsworth scrutinised Dalrymple. 'He would only have been a stripling back then. Who would

211

connect a factory owner with that young student butler?' He lifted an eyebrow. 'Oh, a dragon-hilted sword? Rather showy.'

Dalrymple had pulled the Chippingdales apart. Now he turned to Heddsworth. His lip curled.

'Ah, the famous Heddsworth. The Hall's best swordsman. Miss Regemont's favourite. I don't have a black glove,' he added, referring to the traditional duelling challenge. 'But I can show you how a real butler fights.'

Heddsworth drew his rapier, but someone else stepped forward. It was Fawney, carrying his fireplace poker.

'Beg pardon, Mr Heddsworth,' said Fawney, his raven perched on his shoulder. 'But this is our fight too.'

Dalrymple snorted. 'Have it your way, sweep.' He lifted his sword. Heddsworth stepped back.

Fawney raised his weapon, ashes flying all around him.

Rose was anxious for Fawney. Dalrymple was

a murderous brute while Fawney was a thin, underfed sweep.

But Fawney wielded the poker with perfect expertise. He blocked Dalrymple's strike, and slammed the poker into the side of Dalrymple's leg. Dalrymple let out a gasp of pain. He tried again to stab Fawney, this time aiming for his neck.

Fawney blocked him again and knocked Dalrymple smartly on the head. Dalrymple slid on to the melted snow of the cobblestones, completely unconscious. The raven, cawing, sailed triumphantly into the air.

Watchful appeared on a nearby rooftop, and the raven landed next to him. The bird cawed again, and flapped up to land cheekily on the cat's head. Watchful flicked his tail, and gazed serenely down at the scene below.

A police constable appeared in the light of the dying fire, flanked by his colleagues. 'Stand back, everyone, stand back!' he barked. 'We've an orphanage here burned down! Orphans got out all right? Accident, was it?'

'I believe so,' said Heddsworth. 'However, you may wish to arrest Mr Jabez Cornpepper, otherwise known as Jabez Chippingdale, there, for cruelty and neglect, as well as being an Angelmaker. Am I correct, Miss Raventhorpe? Also Miss Caroline Chippingdale for theft and accessory to murder and kidnapping, and Mr Henry Dalrymple for two counts of murder.'

'How dare you!' cried Caroline. 'You have no proof of such ridiculous accusations!'

'I rather think that Miss Garnet Goldsmith, the Rayburns, a score of orphans, Miss Raventhorpe and the orphanage committee will be able to testify to your wrongdoing, Miss Chippingdale,' replied Heddsworth.

Rose pulled a piece of paper from the front of her dress. It was a page torn from the records Jabez had made. She saw him gawk at it in dismay, but a police constable had seized him by the collar.

Heddsworth nodded to the police constable. 'Quite a haul for you, sir. There should be a promotion by the end of it.'

The constable sucked his moustache, trying not to look pleased. 'Take 'em into custody then,' he ordered his fellows. 'We'll see what a judge and jury make of it all.'

'Get your hands off me,' shrieked Caroline. 'I'm going to rebuild Bleakstone! The Chippingdales will be a great family again!'

Her brother stared at the charred remains of the former mansion as he was handcuffed. 'Can't say I'll miss it,' he muttered.

The Chippingdales and the still unconscious Dalrymple were borne away. Fawney nodded to the butlers, who bowed courteously in return.

Rose went to Fawney. 'Thank you for helping us,' she said. 'You were all extremely heroic.'

'Least we could do,' said Fawney gruffly. 'We're glad to know that it weren't one of your butler friends as did for Mr Wood. Seems Dalrymple was a butler, all right. But he was a proper villain and we went for the wrong man. I want you to know, Miss, we'd have helped you out of the fire whatever 'appened. We wouldn't stand by and let the bairns die.' He turned to Heddsworth. 'What do you say, Mr Heddsworth?'

'I think an end to our hostilities would be excellent,' said Heddsworth. 'None of us will forget what you have done. The Hall and the Society need each other as allies.'

Rose glanced up at the rooftops. The cats, which had been running and stalking about amongst the smoke a few minutes ago, were solid, ordinary statues again.

Rose saw Orpheus staring up at the rooftops.

'Did you see?' she whispered.

Orpheus swallowed. 'Yes,' was all he said.

Rose heard footsteps, and spun round. Bixby had arrived.

'What has happened to Master Herbert?' Bixby demanded. 'Was he in the fire? Was any of this to do with you, Heddsworth? You will be sacked for this, mark my words!'

Bronson eyed Bixby with dislike. 'If you dare do such a thing, I shall challenge you to a duel.'

'I would not duel a woman, Madam,' said Bixby disdainfully.

Charlie Malone grinned. 'Oh, please do.'

'No one is going to duel Bixby,' said Heddsworth. 'He would stand no chance against us.'

Bixby quivered at the insult. 'I shall have you sacked by morning!'

'I suggest you take Master Herbert home for a restoring meal and a hot bath, Bixby,' said Heddsworth. 'It's too cold to stand about here.'

'Fine,' said Herbert sourly. 'I want a complete change of clothes. We'll have to burn these, they're not worth wearing any more.'

Bixby marched him off.

'Pity,' said Bronson. 'I wanted to see you take him down a peg or two.'

One of the Gigg Street people, a wizened old woman, came eagerly forward with a teapot and a few biscuits. 'Poor loves,' she said. 'Summat for you and the bairns.'

Bronson thanked her profusely. The children

broke up the biscuits and shared them. Charlie Malone took the pot of tea, and offered some to the sweeps. 'I don't have many cups, I'm afraid.'

'Not to worry,' said Fawney, and brought a tin cup out of his pocket. 'We'll share.'

Chapter 18

ℬᴵᴿᴰˢ ᴼᶠ ᴬ ℱᴱᴬᵀᴴᴱᴿ

'Have you summoned Orpheus and Inaaya, Heddsworth?' asked Lord Frederick.

He was sitting at the desk in his study while Rose lay on the hearthrug by the fire. She was on her stomach, her feet in the air. Her mother would never let her do such a thing but her father was more lenient. He didn't even mind her new short hairstyle. Lady Constance had expressed her horror in vehement terms. ('Really, Rose! I know you don't want to marry Herbert, but this is going too far! I shall have to buy you a hairpiece!')

'They should be here directly, sir.' Heddsworth poured tea, and arranged mince pies on a Wedgwood china plate. So far he had not been sacked. Bixby and Herbert had tried, but Herbert's complaining telegrams to his father had soured relations between Lord Raventhorpe and the Earl of Dundragan. Bixby had turned sulky, saying that London was a far better place than the barbaric north.

Rose was reading an atlas, working out a route from Yorke to Samarkand across the mountains. It looks easier on paper, Lord Frederick had scoffed. 'You don't know the weather, the people, the politics or the state your own entourage will be in.' So Rose had made up different variables for each, and made calculations. Lord Frederick was pleased with her efforts.

There was a knock at the door and Orpheus entered with Inaaya.

'Oh good. You're here!' Rose exclaimed, jumping to her feet. 'I've been talking to Father and Heddsworth, and we wanted to ask you both something.'

Orpheus nodded uncertainly. 'Do you want us to go to another orphanage? I know there are decent ones in Yorke.'

'No, no, not that at all!' cried Rose.

'Oh no. Of course, the new orphanage for the children is a great improvement on the last,' said Lord Frederick. 'Should jolly well hope so. I've made some decent donations to it. To make sure the children are well cared for, enjoy some outings, that sort of thing.'

'But I thought,' said Rose, 'that you and Inaaya would like somewhere nicer to live. Miss Regemont and the butlers had a long discussion. And they agreed to offer that you two stay at Silvercrest Hall. They have nice rooms there, and Father will sponsor you for your education at a Yorke school if you want it. Even university.'

221

'I'm told you like the idea of being a butler like Bronson, young lady,' said Lord Frederick to Inaaya. 'Splendid idea! Of course, you needn't if you don't want to. You might prefer to become a doctor, something like that. What do you say?'

Orpheus and Inaaya looked at each other.

'Perhaps you'd rather go back to the sailing life,' said Rose anxiously. She would miss Orpheus terribly if he went away, but he and his sister deserved a life of their own.

'You'd really do that for us?' Orpheus glanced from Lord Frederick, to Rose, to Heddsworth.

'Would you like it? You wouldn't be separated,' Rose promised.

Inaaya looked hopefully at Heddsworth.

'Can I learn to fence like Bronson, sir?'

Heddsworth smiled. 'I am sure she will teach you. And your brother.'

'And go to school?'

'If you want to, Miss,' Heddsworth assured her. 'Or learn ballooning, or magic. The Dodge family would love to instruct you in those. The important thing is that you stay together. Do you wish to stay in Yorke?'

Watchful the cat slinked into the room. He perched on the floor and gazed up at Inaaya and Orpheus with golden eyes. Inaaya cooed in recognition, and bent to pick him up.

'He used to visit the orphanage!' she cried. 'He'd come to the window and let us feed him gingerbread.'

Orpheus stared at his sister in astonishment. Rose and Heddsworth smiled. Lord Frederick chuckled indulgently.

'We have to stay,' Inaaya declared. Her arms were full of cat. 'I will stay and be a fighting butler like Bronson.'

'Will the butlers really have us, sir?' Orpheus asked Heddsworth.

Heddsworth looked at the purring Watchful. 'I rather think they will.'

'And if they don't, you can live with us,' promised

Rose. 'We have a dozen spare bedrooms. But you would have to live with Mother, and I think the butlers are a better option.'

'Rose!' chided Lord Frederick.

'I'm sorry, Father.'

'Well, thank you everyone,' said Orpheus at last. 'Including you, Your Lordship.'

'Think nothing of it!' Lord Frederick blushed. 'Always meant to do some such thing. I see far too many unhappy children in this world. Dreadfully dusty in here,' he added, wiping at his eyes. 'I'm going downstairs for a chat with My Lady.'

When Lord Frederick had gone, Orpheus looked worried. 'If we go to the Hall, will we see you, Rose?'

Rose laughed. 'As much as possible. Do you think I'd prefer to spend time with Herbert?'

Orpheus had to grin at that. 'No. But you really want us around?'

'Of course! You're honorary Raventhorpes now.'

'Ha,' said Orpheus. He paused. 'Orpheus Raven is a good nickname. A mix of Rayburn and Raventhorpe.'

'Orpheus Raven,' said Rose. 'Yes, I like that.'

'Like what?' asked Herbert as he came in, scowling. 'Oh, here's Heddsworth! Lazing about again, eh? His days in this house are numbered. What are *they* doing here?' He glared at Inaaya. Inaaya scowled back defiantly. Watchful hissed.

'Oh Herbert,' said Rose sweetly. 'You might like to know that Father is sponsoring Orpheus and Inaaya to live in Yorke. They will be here as our frequent guests.'

Herbert blinked.

'What? You mean, you're engaging them as servants?'

'No,' said Rose. 'They are my friends. Part of the family, really.'

'*What?*'

'Practically adopting them, young sir,' explained Heddsworth.

'Lord Frederick is allowing that – that orphan? Those street urchins – to have the run of the house?'

'Yes,' said Rose happily.

Herbert stared from Rose to the orphans and back again.

'Impossible!'

Orpheus bowed. 'I look forward to sharing the dining table with you, Master Herbert.'

'He's a servant! From the gutter! He's nobody! A piece of muck!'

'Perhaps we should duel for the sake of our honour,' Orpheus suggested. 'How about it, Herbert?'

'It's Master Herbert to you!'

'I suppose this means you don't want me as your best man at the wedding?' said Orpheus.

The future Earl of Dundragan turned purple.

'The wedding,' he spat, 'is *off*.'

With that, Herbert turned on his heel, shouting for Bixby to pack his suitcases. 'We're leaving, right now. They can keep their mad butler. I won't stay here another minute!'

Rose threw her arms around Orpheus and hugged him.

'Anything for my honorary sister,' said Orpheus. 'Merry Christmas.'

The Raventhorpe carriage rolled up to the entrance of Silvercrest Hall. The hall was brilliantly lit for the Butlers' Ball. Orpheus stepped out, dressed in a gorgeous blue and gold coat called a *sherwani*, over soft elegant trousers. Then he chivalrously helped Rose out. Her dress was made from layers of the softest tulle, with a diamond buckle on the satin sash. Madame Vidoux had agreed to change the wedding dress to a ballgown. The cat cameo locket hung around Rose's neck.

'Nice,' said Orpheus, indicating her dress. 'Not too much like a set of curtains.'

Rose made a face at him. 'So says the boy who likes pirate hats.'

Golden Christmas trees lined the entrance. A mist of snow scattered on Rose's wraps. She winced. 'Let's get inside where it's warm!'

They climbed up the steps and through the front door. Miss Regemont welcomed them. She wore a purple velvet gown embroidered with black cats.

'Your sister is waiting for you inside,' said Miss Regemont.

'Thank you, Madam,' said Orpheus, with a graceful bow.

They crossed the threshold of the ballroom. The whole room glowed. Hothouse flowers were arranged in great vases and Christmas trees glittered. An orchestra played on a raised stage.

The orphans had their own private party set up in the adjoining room. The butlers had all chipped in to buy them new clothes for the occasion, and a banquet had been laid out for them on the table. Rose glimpsed a gingerbread house big enough for the smaller ones to climb into. Inaaya, dressed in a gold and scarlet sari, was helping a boy to eat the chimney.

Rose spotted familiar faces among the guests. Harry Dodge had arrived with Emily. Dodge wore his stage attire, including a lined satin cape. Emily wore black and white satin, with the Proops family tiara.

'Miss Regemont invited me herself!' Harry said happily to Rose. 'Terribly kind of her.'

'That's wonderful!' said Rose.

'We're going hot-air ballooning in Scotland soon,' said Emily. 'I can hardly wait. Scotland has such a marvellously mournful atmosphere. All those dark, forbidding lochs and gloomy castles! We shall recite Gothic poetry over the Highlands!'

'I hope you will send me letters,' said Rose.

'Of course! With quotes from tragic poems.'

'You are the queen of all things macabre, my love,' said Dodge fondly. 'Now, where are those orphan children? I'm the star entertainment.' He waved his white-gloved fingers, and a pack of cards appeared.

The ball opened with the Champagne Waltz. Each dancer held a silver tray supporting a filled champagne glass. They danced slowly, without spilling a drop. Then the dance sped up, until they were whirling about at a dazzling rate. Not a splash of champagne left the glasses. When the dance came to an end, the butlers took the glasses from their trays and toasted each other.

'Brilliant!' said Orpheus. Rose clapped until her hands ached.

Next came the Glove Dance. The butlers and their partners circled the ballroom. Each person removed one white glove. The gloves were passed around the room, from dancer to dancer, as they spun by. Miraculously, by the end everyone had their own glove back.

Rose adored the sword dances. The participants swept their rapiers in ever-faster patterns, circling, twirling and striking the blades together in time to the music. The swords glittered in the candlelight.

Next, Bronson and Charlie Malone stepped on to the floor, standing ten feet from each other. Bronson, beautiful in white and silver, carved patterns in the air with her swan-hilted blade. They circled each other, whirling their rapiers. Some of the butlers in the audience played silver tea-trays like drums. The performance ended as the dancers locked swords and bowed. There was a storm of applause.

Charlie Malone smiled at Rose, and gave a little bow. 'It's the only dance I can do without making a mess of it,' he confided. 'Did you bring your rapier, Miss Raventhorpe? No? Here, you can borrow Bronson's.' And they made a sword archway for the dancers to run under. The orphans ran underneath next, giggling.

Orpheus and Rose watched Harry Dodge's conjuring tricks. They ate mince pies and marzipan and fruitcake. When they returned to the ballroom, Heddsworth beckoned to them.

'It's time for the Thousand Diamonds firework display,' said Heddsworth. 'This year the sweeps have created them for us.'

'The sweeps can make fireworks?'

'The Raven Society can,' said Heddsworth. 'It will be good to see their work again.'

They went outside, gladly braving the cold.

The fireworks started with a rain of silver-white stars like snowflakes. Rose joined the gasps of admiration. Next came shimmering golden Christmas trees, and arrows of trailing sparks that crossed in the air like swords. Finally, there was a set piece of fiery, flying birds, and a leaping cat. The birds and cat settled together on a rooftop, and the fireworks gradually flickered away and faded.

Rose smiled. Beyond the firework sparks was the real skyline of the city, its cat statues among them. Rose imagined them watching the fireworks. She twirled her cat cameo in her fingers.

'I thought young Master Orpheus might like a present,' said Heddsworth. 'A gift from Miss Garnet

Goldsmith. Who is wearing her favourite bracelet again. Her father is now allowing her be a proper jeweller.'

He held out a new Infinity Key.

'You can't give me that,' spluttered Orpheus. 'They're for butlers! I know Rose has one, but she's a Raventhorpe.'

'You deserve one,' said Heddsworth. 'You're an honorary Guardian, as much as she is.'

'You absolutely are, Orpheus,' agreed Rose.

Bronson joined them, a vision in silk. 'Oh, you've given him a key,' she observed. 'I hope you know what you're doing, Armand.'

'*Armand?*' said Rose.

Heddsworth turned redder than his glass of wassail punch.

'Ridiculous name,' he muttered. 'It makes me sound like a variety of nut.'

'It's very, um, poetic,' said Rose, stifling her laughter.

'Dignified,' said Orpheus, with a grin.

Watchful the cat prowled out of the shrubbery, and sprang neatly up on to the roof of Silvercrest Hall.

Rose brushed a snowflake out of her eyes. She turned to Orpheus.

'Tomorrow,' she said, 'you're starting fencing lessons.'

Letters from a Hot-Air Balloon

Dearest Rose,

It was lovely to have Orpheus and Inaaya to visit! Inaaya loved the balloon. She is already designing her own, with a new improved gondola. Last week we landed in the grounds of Balmoral Castle, and met her royal Majesty. She was most interested in our mode of transport. In fact she is tempted to buy one herself, painted in the colours of the Victoria tartan. Darling Harry has bought a set of bagpipes. You should hear us from miles away.

Must stop, I am feeling rather queasy. I was sick this morning over the Georgian silver tea service. Our butler was most unimpressed.

Your affectionate friend,
Mrs Emily Dodge

Dear Rose,

Bertram the Second does not like the bagpipes. He growls every time Harry practises. I have to hide them in case he commits an indiscretion on them. (How does one wash a set of bagpipes?)

As you asked, yes, I have been feeling unwell lately. I was sick again this very morning, while reading a book of Gothic Poetry. Fortunately the book was not damaged during the incident. Harry is concerned. I suppose I should cancel my next Poetry and Parasols soiree. It would not do to retch while reciting 'I am half sick of shadows' in The Lady of Shalott.

Yours most affectionately,

Emily Dodge (wife of the renowned Mr H.D.)

Dear Rose,

Really, our dear butler is most unfair. He has asked us to stop playing the bagpipes. He says they are Instruments of War, and should only be played in extraordinary circumstances. ('Entirely desperate circumstances, Madam.') He does not appreciate the beauty and romance of Highland melody.

When I asked for a pickle and jam sandwich, with a serving of peach trifle, he asked me if I had consulted a physician of late. I am sure Heddsworth would not make such peculiar comments. Do come and visit!

Your friend in all things, especially poetry,
Emily

Dearest Rose,

You will never believe it! I am expecting a Happy Event! Harry will be a papa! Our butler is buying baby clothes and cradles and warning me not to go ballooning. It is all splendid. You will be the baby's godmother, I insist.

Now I must consider suitable names. Elfric? Beowulf? Rose the Second? Perhaps I shall add Armand to the list. What do you think of Lancelot? Or Scheherazade?

Harry has suggested 'Harry Heddsworth Spillwell Bronson Malone Dodge.' Joking, I think.

Must go. I am feeling queasy aga . . .

. . . Oh dear. I was sick on the bagpipes.

Fondest love,

Emily Dodge, Mother-to-Be, Balloonist and Admirer of Bagpipes

GLOSSARY

A LIST OF WEIRD WORDS AND FUN FACTS

Mistletoe Service: York Minster's traditional Mistletoe Service really does involve placing mistletoe as well as holly on the altar. The cathedral is unique in this custom, but the reason appears to be lost in time. Whatever the reason, it appeals to me that both plants, rich in history and legend, have their place in the service. The tradition of criminals asking pardon is also a real one. When I read about it, I immediately wanted to include it in Rose's Yorke.

Flinty: The character of Flinty is based on a real Yorkshire person, known as Flint Jack. An alcoholic, he turned to forgery to pay for drink. He sold fake arrowheads, urns and Roman armour around the country.

Angelmakers: Angelmakers really did exist in the Victorian era. They would take in children for care, then do away with them. Some were caught and executed for murder. Unfortunately, it is likely that many were not.

Cat statues: There really are cat statues on buildings in York. Most have been put up quite recently, but they were inspired by much older versions. Legend has it they were meant to scare off vermin from the city.

Skitterways: I called the little alleyways and snickets in the city of Yorke skitterways. I hope this sounds like the skittering of alley cats, ducking from place to place. A twentieth-century author gave the alleys in York the wonderful name of Snickelways. Sadly for me, this name didn't exist in the Victorian era.

Chimney sweeps: The Victorians relied on fires for heating, which meant a lot of work for chimney sweeps. In the early Victorian era, many sweeps hired children to climb up the chimneys and clean them. It was a horrible, dangerous job, and some died in the process. Laws were eventually passed to make child sweeps illegal. Rose lives in the late Victorian era when the practice had ended.

Orphanages: While Victorian orphanages saved children from life on the streets, some had a deservedly bad reputation. Especially the York Industrial Ragged School in Bedern. It was run by George Pimm who hired the children out for such work as chimney sweeping. If a child died, Pimm would hide the body on the school grounds and keep collecting an allowance. As time passed he claimed to be haunted by the spirits of the dead children. The authorities finally took notice and closed the school. Pimm was sent to a lunatic asylum. Tales are still told of ghost children in Bedern.

Mourning dress: After Queen Victoria's husband, Prince Albert, died, she went into mourning for the rest of her life. This made mourning very fashionable and the Victorians did some famously strange things to publicly display their grief. This included hiring mourners at a funeral, wearing black clothing and accessories, and keeping mementoes like the hair of your dead loved one woven into a brooch. The author Charles Dickens enjoyed satirizing the hypocrisy of people who wore 'deep mourning' when they felt no real grief for the departed.

Victorian food: While I have made up Braxton's Baby Food, there were many Victorian foods that could actually make you sick. Arsenic was used as a green dye in some foodstuffs, like sweets. Babies could be given 'medicine' to keep them quiet which might contain gin or opium, which could kill a baby. The poor risked disease and death by using contaminated drinking water, and there was little hygiene in food preparation and storage. Eating in that era could be a very risky business!

Taxidermy: The Victorians loved taxidermy and filled their houses with it. Some of the animals used were killed by hunters and mounted on plaques for the hunter to show off. Others were dearly departed pets. Walter Potter was a famous taxidermist who created whimsical scenes of animals posed in human activities. A prize-winning taxidermist named Edward Allen lived in York in the Victorian era. You can still buy examples of his work.

Slums: Victorian York was full of poverty-stricken people living in slums. Conditions were miserable. The truly destitute had to go to the workhouse.

Slums were overcrowded, cold and dirty, with many families sharing the one toilet. Slum dwellers were lucky to live into their forties. In 1901, Seebohm Rowntree published a book called *Poverty: a Study of Town Life*, exposing the life of the poor in York. Many people had no income or were paid so poorly they could barely keep themselves alive. It helped to shock Britain into social reform.

Acknowledgements

My thanks to the rubies, pearls and all-round gems who helped to shape this book, including my agent Polly Nolan and editor Lena McCauley. Also to Lisa Horton for her stunning cover art, Stephanie Allen, Ashleigh Barton and all the lovely people at Little, Brown UK and Hachette Australia.

Look out for
ROSE RAVENTHORPE
INVESTIGATES
HOUNDS AND HAUNTINGS,
coming in 2018

Lurking in the dead of night
Hell-hound Barghest shuns the light.
Sharp of fang and red of eye
he will stalk you till you die...